He was convinced the battle of Waterloo made him half a man...until he met her

Daniel Sinclair is a broken man with wounds that are physical and spiritual. He's weighed down by grief and guilt that he could not save his friend, Graeme Lennox, and is convinced that a French lance left him less than a man. He has no prospects. Nothing left but his tarnished honor. But then he meets a vexing boy who makes him question even that.

Fia Lennox's world turned on its end with her brother's death. She's gone in one fell swoop from lady to servant...to a woman on the run. The world is a dangerous place for a woman alone—even when she's masquerading as a boy—so when she meets up with a strong, valiant ex-cavalryman, she decides to become his traveling companion. Whether he likes it or not.

Battling villains, would-be-friends and their own finely-forged battlements, Fia and Daniel rush toward their destiny, a scorching passion and, hopefully, redemption. Can love conquer all? Even the ghosts of the past?

TARNISHED HONOR

SABRINA YORK

Tarnished Honor
ISBN #: 978-1-941497-16-6
©Copyright Sabrina York 2015
Cover Design by Dar Albert
Edited by Carrie Jackson

TARNISHED
HONOR

Dedication

This book is dedicated to Cerise, who made it happen.

CHAPTER ONE

Daniel Sinclair shot up with a gasp. His heart pounded in his throat. Sweat prickled his brow. Skitters of horror danced on his nape. It took far too long for his brain to realize he was not ankle-deep in the blood-soaked field of battle. That the whinnying of the horses in the stable below was a far cry from the screams of dying men. The patter of the rain on the roof was not the thundering echoes of a thousand hooves battering the ground as a division of inexperienced cavalrymen charged the French infantry. The rapping on the door was not the staccato retort of countless muskets in a melee of agony and death.

The scorching fire in his leg, however, was real.

He shouldn't have moved so quickly. One day, hopefully one day soon, he would remember in time. He was not a whole man. He never would be again.

Damn that dream anyway.

But it wasn't a dream. Not really.

The knock on the door came again. "Sinclair? Sinclair? Are you in there?"

"Aye. I'll be right out." He gingerly readjusted his leg, searching for a position where it didn't ache. He did not find one. One would think, after nine months, his wound wouldn't still be so tight. The muscles would have healed, the ligaments reconnected. The pain would have lessened.

The doctors told him, time and time again, how lucky he was. That he could have lost his leg when a French lance ripped through his upper thigh. Had it nicked an artery, he would have bled out, right there on the field, as so many had.

Lucky.

So lucky.

The doctors were idiots.

If he *had* been lucky, he *would* have bled out that day, on the field outside the charming Belgian village of Waterloo. Then he would have been a dead hero, like Ponsonby and Lennox and so many others. He wouldn't be half a man, a crippled veteran—of his first and only battle, no less—struggling to survive on a modest pension and the charity of his compatriots.

One of whom was awaiting him now.

He pulled on his trousers and boots, as well as a clean shirt, and limped to the door. Paul Beaufort, Earl of Sherstone and one of the founders of the club that had hired Daniel, stood on the landing. Despite the late hour—or the early hour depending on one's perspective—he looked as fresh as a man who had just awoken. But then, he always did. He was called "Lucky" by his men because, unlike most of them, he'd never suffered any serious injury throughout the Peninsula Campaign or at Waterloo. He was tall, with short dark hair and warm brown eyes. His lips curled into an apologetic smile when he saw Daniel.

"Sorry to bother you," he said. "I just arrived."

"Not a problem, my lord." Daniel closed the door behind him and followed Sherstone down to the stables, where a beautiful stallion patiently awaited a currying.

Daniel quickly removed its saddle and tackle and began drying the horse off.

Sherstone helped, though he didn't need to; it was hardly his job. "It was a miserable ride, I must say. All that rain," he said as he fed his horse a handful of oats.

"Aye, my lord."

The earl's snort, rounding the room as it did, surprised him. "You don't need to *my lord* me, Sinclair. We've been through far too much together for such formality."

Daniel couldn't help but smile. Sherstone had always been a good sort, treating each and every man as though he had value—no matter what. Many British lords were not so gracious.

"I appreciate that, Sherstone. I do. But we're no' on the battlefield now, are we? In London, you are a lord and I am a groom. And..." He waggled a curry brush at his friend. "Bluidy glad to be one."

When a group of peers, who had served at Waterloo, had opened this club, they'd made it a priority to hire veterans. And thank heaven they had. Without this job Daniel would have nothing—not so much as a roof over his head—and he damned well appreciated the salvation.

Sherstone nodded. "I understand. But...when we're alone, you should call me Paul." He thrust out a hand and Daniel took it. Paul's grip was firm and solid. Warm.

"Aye...Paul. I will."

"Oh, thank God."

"You go on. I can finish here. You must be tired."

"Yes, I daresay I am. Perhaps I will see you tomorrow, Sinclair?" Sherstone asked.

Daniel held back his laugh. "Aye. I'll be here." Where else would he be? This stable was his life now. Its confines drew the perimeter of his world. This was now all there was. All there ever could be.

He had no idea why that thought sent a spiral of despair through him.

When he woke in the morning, the first thing he saw was the chess piece on his bedside table—a beautiful hand-carved knight, hewn of darkened wood. It sent a sliver of familiar anguish through him.

He should move it somewhere else so he wouldn't have to look at it every day. Hide it. Throw it away.

Hell, what he should do was deliver it to its rightful owner, send the girl the damned piece and exorcize Lennox from his soul forever, but for some reason, he couldn't let it go. It was all he had left. Besides, how could he face her? How could he explain?

How could he tell the girl her brother was dead because of him?

With a snarl, he rose from the bed and dressed, deliberately avoiding the mirror hanging on the wall. He didn't like what he saw in that murky surface. The man he had become.

He was a killer. A man so weighted with guilt he should barely be able to lift his head. How many men had he sent to perdition with his saber? A hundred? A thousand? He had no idea. That was the darkest part of it.

Nay. Untrue. The darkest part of it was it had all happened in one day. One drizzly, rainy day.

He hadn't killed anyone else, not a soul, in all of his twenty-nine years. Over ten thousand five hundred days where he'd managed to pass the time without so much as slaughtering anyone.

This did not make him less of a killer.

This did not make it any easier to look at himself in the glass. It didn't make it any easier to shake off the specters of the past.

How they wailed within him.

He plodded slowly down the stairs, favoring his left leg, and checked on the horses before heading to the kitchen for breakfast. Though he took his time with each and every mount, he spent a little more with Hunnam, his own horse. One of the reasons Daniel had been so grateful for this position was that Sherstone and Colonel Worth had agreed to allow him to stable his horse on the premises. Otherwise, he would have had to sell his Grey, and that would have killed him.

Hunnam was a magnificent beast, well-trained and strong. Daniel had had several offers for him, but the stallion had saved his life more than once. He wasn't a piece of property to Daniel. He was his friend.

It occurred to him he might want to revise his opinion when Hunnam greeted him with an exhalation that dampened his shirt. He could hardly blame the beast for his insolence. He was probably bored and frustrated. It was a damn shame Daniel didn't get much time to ride him—a worse shame that more than once, with his weak leg, he'd been thrown. But several members of the club were more than happy to take the warhorse out for exercise at every opportunity.

They were a good lot, the members of the Incomparables Club. Daniel was lucky to call them his friends. Hell, he was just plain lucky.

He didn't feel so lucky when he walked into the kitchen to find Fanny lying in wait.

Fanny was one of the few females the members of the club had hired. She served as chambermaid and occasionally assisted Brodie, the cook, in the kitchen. For some reason, she had decided Daniel was the man of her dreams.

Her attentions filled him with horror.

Oh, she was a beauty, to be sure, with flowing red hair and a sweet smile. Her body had all the curves a man could ask for, and more. Beyond that, it was clear she found Daniel attractive—although why, in his condition, he couldn't fathom.

Before the war he would have welcomed her attentions with open arms. But now? Now she terrified him.

It wasn't that she was ungainly or bucktoothed or ill-mannered. She was none of those things.

It was the fact that, when he looked at her, he felt...nothing.

When a man looked at a woman that beautiful, that curvy, that welcoming, there should be a warmth somewhere in his belly. A trickle of interest.

Hell, there should be lust. A raging firestorm of it.

But there was no lust in Daniel's heart. Nor in any other nook or cranny of his body or soul. And there had not been for nearly a year. He despaired he would ever feel it again.

That was the worst part of all this. Worse than surviving when so many of his friends had not. Worse than the memories that refused to release their hold on him. Worse than the despair that sometimes clawed at his soul. Worse than the ever-present pain in his leg.

The reality that he was a shadow of his former self.

Half a man.

And Fanny reminded him of that, each and every time he looked at her. She reminded him of what he had once been. Of what he no longer was. For in truth, since that bloody dismal June day in Belgium, he hadn't felt a stir of attraction for any woman.

"There he is," she cooed as he stepped into the kitchen.

The smell of ham and eggs assailed him and his stomach growled. He nodded to Brodie and then to Fanny. "Good morning."

"Good morning, darling." She sashayed over to him, her hips swaying. Her bosom was full. Her expression was warm. He should have felt...*something*. But he didn't. There was nothing. "Don't you look fine?"

He had no idea how to respond to that. He didn't know how he looked—avoiding the mirror and all—but he was certain it wasn't *fine*. When he turned away, to take a plate from Brodie and sit at the table, she put out a lip and sat opposite him.

"I was thinking maybe you and I could go for an outing on your next day off." She fluttered her lashes, as though that would add to her appeal. It did not.

She was appealing enough already.

"I doona take days off."

She affected a shudder. "Och, I do love a brogue." She propped her chin on her hand and gazed at him. "Say something else."

He gaped at her. "What?"

"Anything. Anything."

"I doona know what to say."

She tipped back her head and gusted, "Yes, yes," as though the sound of his voice sent her into raptures.

Behind her, at the stove, Brodie rolled his eyes. "Don't you have work to do, missy?" he grumbled. Brodie was not a man of many words, so Daniel appreciated the effort on his behalf.

Fanny shot a glare over her shoulder. Brodie met it with one of his own. Brodie's glare won. She blew out a heavy sigh and stood. Then she pinned Daniel with a flirtatious smile and purred, "I'll see you later, Daniel." She made it a point to cross behind him as she exited the room, dragging her fingers over his shoulders.

When she was gone, Daniel let go a breath. "Thank you," he said to Brodie.

"Bah, that one," the crusty old cook growled. "Best keep your distance or she'll eat you alive." No doubt. "Ah. Just so's you know, Colonel Worth is looking for you," he added.

"Colonel Worth?"

"Aye. I believe he's in the morning room."

"Thank you." Daniel finished his breakfast and set the plate with the others to be washed and then nodded to Brodie before heading through the hall to find Drayton Worth, Baron Lansdowne. He wasn't difficult to find, not with that red hair. Aside from that, he was the only one in the morning room at this hour.

Worth had been a colonel in the Royal Artillery, a nobleman of ancient lineage who'd purchased a commission at seventeen, but he and Daniel had met many times before they found themselves fighting together on a battlefield in Belgium. They'd been friends for years.

"There you are," Worth said as he spotted Daniel. He folded his ironed paper and waved to a chair.

Daniel sat, though he was uncomfortable doing so; he was quite aware of his station, even if his friends seemed inclined to ignore it.

"You wanted to see me?"

"Indeed. A letter came for you with the morning's post." He slid the parchment across the table.

Daniel frowned. A letter? There was no one to write him. His father had died when he was a boy and his mother had succumbed to the ague when he'd been a young man. And other than Sherstone and Worth and a precious few others, his friends had perished on the Continent.

He studied the envelope—an address in Inverness, one he didn't recognize—and then slid his finger beneath the flap.

The contents of the letter left him even more perplexed. He stared at it in shock.

"What is it?" Worth asked.

"My uncle has died."

"My condolences."

Daniel snorted. "None necessary. He was a hard-hearted old bastard." He would never forgive Uncle William's silence when Daniel had pleaded with him to help his mother. A few pennies could have eased her misery. A few more for medicine could have saved her life. But William had been too tightfisted even for that.

Aside from which, William had always deplored Daniel. It was so inconvenient when one's brother married beneath the family standard. And an Irish woman to boot.

A familiar fury curled within him and Daniel crumpled the paper into a ball.

Worth tipped his head to the side. "I take it you and your uncle weren't close?" Humor threaded his tone.

"Not in the slightest."

"Who sent the letter then?"

"His solicitors."

"That is interesting."

"Apparently he's left me something. They're asking me to come to Inverness and meet with them."

Worth chuckled. "I take it from your tone you're not tempted to comply."

"Inverness is a long way away."

"That it is."

Daniel smoothed out the paper. "Knowing Uncle William, it willna be worth the journey." The title and the estate would go to William's son, Fergus, and anything of value beyond that would go to his other cousin, the one William had favored. It was highly unlikely he would have left anything to Daniel, the boy he'd once called a mongrel. If anything, this bequest would be a cruel jibe or a further insult to his heritage.

On the other hand, how satisfying would it be to throw this inheritance, whatever it was, back in William's face?

Of course William was dead. He probably wouldn't notice. But it would still be damned satisfying. A vindication. A statement of Daniel's utter contempt.

"I think you should go," Worth said.

Daniel shook his head. "I doona want to give up my position here so I can spend a month or more gallivanting around the country."

Worth clapped him on the shoulder. "You will always have a position here, Daniel. Surely you know that."

"There are many other men who need work." The countryside was littered with war veterans, broken and broke.

"Yes. And one of them can fill in for you until you return. I think you should go. It would do you good."

Daniel recognized the look in Worth's eyes, the shadows. The guilt and regret and the ache for things to be as they once were.

Good God. How wonderful would it be to ride again? Take to the open road and *ride*? It was who he was. Who he had been at the very least. It certainly was who he wanted to be once again. In truth, Daniel yearned to feel his mount between his thighs once more. To feel the wind whipping through his hair. To grasp at some small piece of what had been Daniel Sinclair, valiant, daring cavalryman.

Aye, maybe a journey was just what he needed.

CHAPTER TWO

FIA LENNOX SHIVERED AS SHE WASHED HER HANDS IN the icy bucket, scrubbing away the grunge from the kitchen grate. She hated Tuesdays, because the staff was expected to do the deeper cleaning in addition to all their other tasks. And her day was full as it was, tending to the needs of the wealthy daughters of Scotland's elite at Dunready's School for Ladies. Some of them were rather demanding.

It mortified her a bit that she had once been one of them.

Well, she wasn't anymore.

At any rate, Tuesdays were difficult. Every muscle ached as she finally made her way up the narrow stairs to the cold garret room on the top floor. She nearly grimaced as she pushed open the door and caught sight of the hard, lumpy mattress awaiting her, but she didn't. She didn't even have the energy for that.

She dropped down and draped her arm over her eyes to block out the light of the moon shining through the grimy window. It had been a grueling day.

They all were, nowadays. She was up before the dawn and didn't finish until hours after all the girls had gone to bed.

She didn't even bother to undress before she collapsed. Honestly, there didn't seem to be a point. Too soon she would have to rise again. And it wasn't as though her clothing mattered. She was a servant now, and probably would be until the day she died.

Everything she owned—except for the precious carvings her brother had made for her—had been gifts from others. The blanket that kept her from freezing had been smuggled to her by Chelsea. The candles she used, on the odd occasion she had energy to light them, were stubs given to her by others. Even the food she ate—beyond the porridge the servants were served—was slipped into her pockets by her erstwhile friends.

How funny it was that life could turn so capriciously.

Fia had been born to wealth and privilege, the sister of a lord, sent to one of the finest finishing schools in Perth. Only now did she curse how very fine—and expensive—it had been.

When catastrophe had descended and the money for her tuition and board had stopped coming, Blackbottom, the school's headmistress, had confiscated Fia's things—every dress, every shoe, every book—and sold them all to pay her debt. Even her horse, Tilly, and the necklace her mother had left her, had gone on the block. Sadly, it was not enough to cover all she owed.

Blackbottom had been kind when she'd shared the news with Fia, just as she had when she'd passed on the news of Graeme's death. And the news that Fia's uncle—who had inherited Graeme's estate and the title—had refused to continue paying for her keeping.

Aye, Blackbottom had been kind when she explained to Fia that she was now alone in the world. That her debt to the school was extensive and it was only right that she work it off.

She was kind when she offered Fia a home here—albeit in the garret.

She was kind when she reminded Fia that she hadn't anywhere to go. Not now. Not with Graeme dead and her home gone.

So kind when she explained that the life Fia had always known, the expectations she'd had—of love and marriage and children—the hopes and dreams and prospects she'd once treasured, had all died with her brother.

Blackbottom had always been so kind.

On the surface at least.

Fia knew better now. She saw the darkness beneath that serene and polished façade. She saw the nasty woman none of the other girls would ever see. She'd felt the fall of the cane when she displeased her mistress.

She hated that she had to stay here but there was nowhere else to go.

It was a stunning realization, how huge the chasm was between the servant and the privileged class. If she had not lived it, Fia would never have believed the world could be so cruel.

She knew now, it could be.

The doorknob jiggled, shattering her dismal thoughts.

Fia shot up and stared at it through the shadows. The hair on her neck prickled. Sweat, cold and clammy, blossomed on her brow.

Damn. Damn, damn.

She'd been so woozy, she'd forgotten to latch the door. How could she ever have forgotten?

Her heart lurched into her throat as the knob turned and the door creaked open. A large shadow loomed.

She knew exactly who it was—even if her humming instincts hadn't screamed it, even if she hadn't expected him to try this again. In truth, she should have smelled him coming.

Blackbottom's nephew, Horace, was known for skulking about the female servants' quarters at night. He'd attacked more than one girl, though the headmistress had taken it into her head to blame the girls for being loose. Horace was petulant, a pestilence. A boil on the butt of humanity.

How on earth had she forgotten to lock the door?

She swallowed, though her throat ached. Her pulse throbbed in her forehead. Her gaze raked the shadows, desperately searching for something, some weapon. Some way to protect herself.

There was nothing.

She had nothing.

Nothing but a carved chess set she kept hidden beneath the floorboards, and those precious pieces would hardly prove lethal.

"Well, hullo, missy." His chuckle slithered through the room, making it feel even colder than it was. His eyes glinted in the moonlight. His tongue darted out like a snake's.

"Go away," she snarled, trying to make her voice as mean as she could. She doubted that would help. He probably liked mean. She eased up out of bed—probably not the best place to face a man like this—and edged to the other side of the chamber, though it was a tiny chamber; his gaze tracked her.

"I'm not going anywhere." His lips lifted in a smirk. "You and I are going to have a...chat."

He stepped into the doorway, nearly filling it, but Fia noticed a small gap. Surely it was large enough for her to slip through, if she moved quickly.

She decided to make a try—hopefully she could catch him off guard—and lunged forward. He was, apparently, experienced in the desperate ploys of women he had cornered, for he grabbed her arm and yanked her toward him. He did so with such force, she flew back and stumbled and then, oh horrors, tumbled to the floor.

He was on her in a second, covering her and crushing her and suffocating her with his mouth. His breath was fetid, his touch repulsive. Fia lashed from side to side, but it did no good. Horace was far too sturdy. She couldn't throw him off. He made revolting, piggish sounds as his hands roved and then, to her dismay, he tugged up her skirts. When they didn't lift quickly enough, he ripped them open.

The tearing sound echoed, twined with her cry of dismay. Not only was she certain Horace was going to rape her, right here and now, he'd just ruined her only dress. The only thing she had to wear in the entire world.

Fury savaged her. Oh, if only she had a weapon. Even a butter knife would do.

A pity there was no butter knife handy, but from the corner of her eye, she spotted something beneath the bed.

Something that was always beneath the bed. Something she would never even have thought of, had she not been so utterly desperate.

The chamber pot.

As Horace rooted in the tattered material of her dress, searching for something to ravage, Fia reached out, farther and farther, until her fingers found the cold hard pottery.

As he leaned up, to fumble with the ties to his breeks, she lifted the heavy pot and clouted him on the side of the head. His eyes flared and he fixed her with a surprised look, and then, with a groan, he crumpled to the floor in a lifeless lump.

Fia studied him, looking for some evidence she hadn't killed him. She poked him with a finger. He didn't move.

Oh dear, oh dear.

She'd done it now.

When Blackbottom found out, she'd have Fia hanged.

The thought, the implications of this debacle sat like a stone on her soul. She had to leave. Had to run.

She wasted little time packing her things. Indeed, there was little to pack. She pried up the board in the floor—which, thankfully, Horace had not landed upon—and pulled out her one treasure, the hand-carved chess set Graeme had made for her while in France. He'd created and sent them to her, one piece at a time. It had been their connection while he'd been away. His promise. Each piece reminding her he would be home again soon. Again, they would play.

Sadly, the set was not complete. Never would be. One man was missing. But she treasured it, because it was all she had left of him. All she had left of her brother.

Without a glance back at her dreary room, Fia headed into the hall and crept down the creaky stairs to the lavish third floor, where the students had their quarters. While she knew she shouldn't tarry—if he was not dead, Horace could awaken at any time—she couldn't leave without saying good-bye to her best friend.

She and Chelsea had been like two peas in a pod since they'd met, young girls shuttled away from home to be properly groomed for marriage. Of all the girls at Dunready's, they'd been the least suited for marriage. Or grooming. They'd bonded immediately and become the best of friends. Both were hellions to the core. They'd spurred and inspired each other's mischief. And of all the friends she'd had here, Chelsea was the one who had stayed faithful when Fia's circumstance came crumbling down.

Both their brothers had been members of the Scots cavalry, the infamous Scots Greys. They'd huddled together in prayer for their brothers as news trickled in about the battles of the war. And when the devastating report of

Graeme's death had come, Chelsea had been the one to hold her, comfort her, keep her soul alive through that horrific time.

Not that it still wasn't horrific, but the burden was easier to bear. She'd adjusted to his loss. At least, as best she could. It wasn't as though she had a choice.

One either adjusted, or one curled into a ball and died.

She was not curling into a ball.

Graeme would have hated that.

Nae, she hadn't given up then, and she would not give up now. She would embrace this new adventure—whatever it was—with open arms. Indeed, it felt oddly freeing.

But then, she supposed, escape often did.

Chelsea opened her door at first knock. No doubt she'd been reading. She often did, late into the night. She greeted Fia with a smile, but when she took in her state of dishevelment, her smile faded. "Fia. Come in."

"I'm sorry to bother you at this hour," Fia said as she stepped into Chelsea's room. She couldn't resist a glance over her shoulder. No one was there. Of course they weren't.

"I don't mind," Chelsea said. "I've told you so a thousand times. But..." Her nose wrinkled. "What is that smell?"

Fia ignored the question and took her friend by the hand. There wasn't a moment to lose. "Something's happened, Chelsea. I need to leave here at once."

Chelsea blinked at her panicked tone. "Whatever has happened?"

"I think I killed him." Fia knew she was in something of an uproar, but it had been a trying night.

"Killed whom?" Chelsea asked as though such a turn of events didn't startle her in the slightest. And as though there were numerous prospects to choose from.

"Horace."

"Och. Him." Chelsea shuddered. "What happened?"

"He came to my rooms. He... He tried to... I hit him over the head."

"With what?"

Fia's lashes fluttered. "The chamber pot."

Chelsea studied her. Her nose wiggled a little once more. "Was it empty or full?"

A cringe. "Half and half."

"I see."

No doubt, she *smelled* as well.

"But I might have killed him, and even if I haven't...I need to leave. Now. And I couldn't do so without saying good-bye and..."

"And?"

"Asking if I could borrow some clothes." She gestured to the rags she wore.

Chelsea huffed a breath. "Those do reek." She headed to her wardrobe and began to riffle. "Wherever shall you go?"

Fia's heart thumped. "I haven't a clue. Just away."

"What nonsense." An item flew out. And another. "You have to have a plan."

A plan would be wonderful. A pity she didn't have one.

She opened her mouth to respond, but Chelsea didn't give her a chance. "You shall go to Wick."

"To Wick?"

"It is the only sensible option. Charles will take care of you." Fia nearly groaned. For years, Chelsea had insisted that one day Fia and her brother would fall in love and marry, and then the two girls would be sisters forever. It was a charming scenario, for a fantasy, and it might have borne fruit, if Fia's circumstances had not shifted so sharply. She had nothing to offer this magnificent and heroic Charles of whom Chelsea so incessantly spoke. Nothing.

"I canna impose upon Lord Wick."

"Pish. It is hardly an imposition."

"He willna want me hanging about." No wellborn lord with a title and a castle wanted to be saddled with a penniless waif. Who smelled of offal.

Chelsea whirled and grabbed Fia's hands. "It's not an imposition," she hissed intently. "If roles had been reversed, and Charles had died instead of Graeme, you would do the same for me."

Fia's lips worked. She couldn't deny it. It was the truth. She would do anything for Chelsea. "But...Wick is so far from here. However will I get there?"

"You shall take Blaze."

Fia gaped. "Blaze? I canna take your horse." Chelsea loved that horse. Blaze was her favorite thing on earth. She would be lost without her.

"Nonsense. She will enjoy the journey. She doesna get near enough exercise as it is. Besides, it takes forever in post chaises. Aside from that, when you leave here, Blackbottom will be looking for you. It would be best if you take the back roads and..." She eyed Fia up and down. "You canna go looking like that." She waved a dainty hand.

"Like what?"

"A woman."

Fia blew out a breath. "I am a woman."

"Exactly!" Chelsea turned back to her search. She pulled something from the bottom of a drawer and tossed it on the bed. And then something else. Fia picked up the items and held them out, her mind spinning with incredulity. They weren't ladies' clothes. They weren't decent. Chelsea caught her expression. "If you're going on the run, you canna travel as Fia."

"Can I not?"

"Doona be ridiculous. It's far too dangerous. Put these on." She thrust the garments into Fia's arms. A pair of breeches and a rough-hewn shirt.

"Where did you get these?"

"I stole them."

"You stole them?"

"From the line."

"Why on earth would you steal these?"

Chelsea nibbled her lip and shrugged. "I might have been planning an insurrection. At the very least, it seemed logical that they would come in handy. And you see? They have." Her smile was dazzling, but then it always was. She fingered Fia's long, thick curls. "Blackbottom won't be looking for a boy." She held up a pair of shears; the gleam in her eye was a trifle disturbing.

Fia lurched away. "Egads. You're no' cutting my hair."

"Do you want to escape?"

"Of course I do."

"Then we shall do what is necessary."

Fia squeezed her eyes closed, trying not to wince at the heinous snips. She felt her hair falling but couldn't bear to watch. But when Chelsea cooed, she had to peep. She cracked open a lid and glanced at the mirror and…oh heavens. It didn't look like her. It didn't look like her at all. With her hair closely cropped, her cheekbones were suddenly more prominent, her eyes wider and her neck exposed. Short, dark curls clung to her scalp in a rakish tumble. She was not displeased.

She shot her friend a grin. "I doona look like myself at all now."

"Nae, you don't." Chelsea fluffed her hair.

"I look like…a boy!"

"Exactly! This way you can travel safely to Wick."

"Charles willna even recognize me." They'd only met a few times, and only in passing, but he would never believe she was his sister's friend.

"Nonsense. I shall write you a letter to give him. Come. We must hurry."

Chelsea escorted her through the echoey halls to the kitchen and helped her gather some food. And then—with the letter to Charles, a handful of coins Chelsea had saved from her pin money, and the chess pieces that had been Graeme's last gift to her tucked in her bag—Fia mounted Chelsea's magnificent white charger and rode off into the night. To her future.

Who knew what tomorrow would hold?

She could only hope it wasn't disaster.

CHAPTER THREE

GLORIOUS.

There was no other word for it. Simply glorious.

Daniel tipped his face up to the sky and grinned. The sun was shining and the breeze was mild. The sky was blue and tufted with fat white clouds. It was a lovely day to travel—it could have been raining, could have been cold. But since he'd set out from London, on this lengthy journey to Inverness, each day had been prettier than the last.

His mood had improved too. He was swamped with the conviction that he'd done the right thing, leaving his haven. As much as he appreciated his position at the club, he'd allowed himself to sink into it, into the rut of it. He'd allowed himself to wallow in his woes.

There was no wallowing on the road; there simply wasn't time for it.

It was energizing to be traveling again, invigorating to be out in the world, breathing fresh air and going somewhere. He enjoyed the solitude, the quiet, the absence of need to make conversation.

That left him alone with his thoughts, his regrets and his guilt of course, but such specters had haunted him for so long, they were like old companions. He wouldn't know who he was without them.

Aye. This was far more healing than any medicine — the power of his mount between his thighs, the kiss of warmth on his face, the movement. Surprisingly, his leg hardly pained him at all, except when he moved suddenly. In fact, it even felt better after several days of riding. He hadn't fallen off his horse once.

Hunnam was in good form as well. No doubt he'd enjoyed the fresh air and the chance to prance once again. An hour's exercise a day was one thing, but for a Scots Grey, the chance to run and run wild spoke to his soul.

It spoke to Daniel's too, so he put his heels to his mount's sides and gave him his head.

And it was glorious.

He hadn't realized how closed up he'd allowed himself to become. How isolated. He hadn't realized how much he'd allowed his injury — and his guilt — to shrink his horizons.

Well, his horizons weren't limited now. They spread before him in a verdant green wash that stretched as far as the eye could see. He passed a loch and paused to admire the sparkling waters, to watch an osprey swoop down to snatch a hapless fish.

And damn, but it was a fine thing to be back in Scotland. Daniel hadn't realized just how much he'd missed hearing the lilt of his own brogue, or tasting a well-made haggis. The Brits didn't care for haggis, a fact he'd never quite understood. When created by someone who knew what they were doing, it was delicious. And Scottish innkeepers, apparently, knew what they were doing. Or their wives did.

There was no doubt about it, he'd probably gained a stone since crossing the border to his homeland. He'd never felt so vibrant and alive. And while he had enjoyed the occasional chat with a fellow countryman, he'd never enjoyed his own company more. There was something about being alone with one's thoughts that was very peaceful. It allowed a man to explore his soul at leisure without interruptions. It allowed a man to process all that had happened in his life. To put everything in the place it belonged. Though he still had several days of travel, at most a week, he was already lamenting the journey's end.

After he passed the Kinclaven Crossroads, the landscape changed from fields and farms to orchards. The looming trees shaded the road in a lacy pattern; the scent of crisp apples filled the air, tempting Daniel to reach up and pluck one for a taste.

He did not. That would be stealing and he was a man of honor.

He pulled back on Hunnam's reins when he spotted a white mare standing in the road. She was difficult to miss. Her lines were exquisite, her saddle and tack were the finest...but she had no rider. His brow wrinkled as he rode closer. No one would ever abandon such a fine horse. It was—

"Blast."

The imprecation came from the leafy tree next to which the mare stood.

Daniel glanced up; the boughs riffled. An apple fell to the ground.

The mare whinnied and walked over to it, lipping up the treat.

Another apple fell and the horse made short work of that one was well.

"Stop eating them all," the tree said. "Save some for me."

Daniel cleared his throat. It seemed prudent to make himself known. "Hullo?"

The leaves rustled and a face peered out. Enormous blue-green eyes stared at him. Something flickered through them. Something that could have been construed as...guilt.

Daniel frowned. "What are you doing up there?" he asked.

The eyes blinked. "Nothing."

"Nothing?" He drummed his fingers on his saddle. "Are you stealing apples?"

The chagrined expression on that elfin face was nearly whimsical. "Is this your orchard?"

"Indeed it is not."

An entrancing, mischievous smile blossomed and the thief tossed him a fat red apple. "Then catch."

He did not. He did not catch. The apple bounced off his pate.

"Oh really," an amused voice echoed from above. "Let's try again."

"Let's not."

Too late. Another apple flew in his direction. He missed it again. It fell to the ground and Hunnam gobbled it up.

"Sir, you are supposed to catch them."

"I doona care to abet you in your thievery —" Another missile flew. By the grace of God, he caught this one. "Please stop throwing stolen apples at me." It was large and red and shiny and looked delicious. Aside from that, it smelled quite tantalizing. As he felt he had earned it, he polished it on his lapel and took a bite. Flavor exploded in his mouth and juice dribbled down his chin. They were excellent apples.

The face disappeared, followed by more rustling. A satchel fell to the loam with a soft thud. Then a pair of feet appeared. Legs. Slim hips. Slender shoulders and then a mop of tousled black curls.

A boy dropped to the ground with an oof. He looked up at Daniel, his head tipped saucily to the side, and then he grinned. It was a rakish grin. "Not stealing. Borrowing."

This he said with such conviction, Daniel had to struggle not to laugh. This was no laughing matter. Thieves ended up in the gaol. "Ah. Borrowing. Surely you won't mind explaining that to him." Daniel nodded to the distance, where a farmer was running through the trees toward them, arms flailing.

The boy's eyes widened. He picked up the satchel and hefted it over his shoulder. Then he bounded into his saddle and shot a glance back at Daniel. His grin was wicked as he urged his mount forward...leaving Daniel behind to explain to the farmer why his apples were missing.

He paid for them. He had to. The evidence was still running down his chin. Once he had calmed the farmer with a collection of coins, he set his heels to Hunnam's sides and continued on. He didn't intend to catch up with the little thief, but he did. The boy was waiting for him at a turn in the road.

"That was clever of you," he said as he came abreast of the white mare.

The boy shot him a curious glance. "Clever?"

"Making me your accomplice."

"Ah." The boy looked away, but Daniel saw his smile. "Are you blaming me for your lack of self-discipline?"

Daniel bristled. "I'm verra self-disciplined."

"Are you?"

He didn't care for the way the urchin looked him up and down, as though his willpower were in question. He was a soldier. He was known for his iron will. The dubious appraisal nudged Daniel to say, "I was not the one pilfering apples."

"Borrowing."

"Right. And when, precisely, do you intend to return them?"

His small chin jutted out. "I will."

"When?"

The glance the boy shot Daniel might have been a wounded one. "When I can," he said softly.

For some reason, the words shafted through him and sliced deep. He remembered being a boy with no means. He remembered the hunger and the worry. He'd never stolen apples, but he might have. Which was probably why he muttered, "Don't worry. I paid the farmer."

The boy sighed. "Thank you." He peeped a look at Daniel. "Would you like some of them? It only seems right. Since you paid for them." There was a hesitancy to the offer that made Daniel wonder if the apples were all that stood between this child and a hungry night. Which, in turn, made him feel like a louse.

"Maybe later." A grumble. He had no idea why it elicited a glowing smile.

Good glory, he was large. Fia felt like a mite riding next to him. But despite how large he was, and intimidating in his manner, he didn't frighten her, even when he scowled. Perhaps it was the indulgent tweak of his lips as he'd watched her harvest the apples. Or perhaps it was the fact that he'd paid for her sins. Or maybe it was just that look in his eye.

Or the fact that he was riding a grey horse. Graeme had ridden a Grey.

It might be naive to trust him simply because he seemed to be a military man and his horse so resembled those of her brother's regiment—or because of his fascinating eyes—but

Fia felt certain she could. And he had welcomed her into his company. Well, not welcomed so much as…tolerated.

Granted, she hadn't given him much choice—she'd simply followed him—but then she'd had little choice herself. She knew now what folly it was to travel alone, even pretending to be male. Even males were not safe alone in this world.

It hadn't taken long for her vulnerability to ring out. Hadn't taken long for a predator to find her.

Less than a day after leaving Perth, she'd been robbed. As she slept that night in the stable of the first inn she'd stayed at, a blackheart had stolen all her belongings. Her money, certainly, but more. He'd stripped her of the chess set Graeme had made for her.

Even now, the memory of waking up to find her things gone—along with the young man with whom she'd shared the loft—sent her pulse rocketing through her. Aside from Horace's visit, it had been the most horrifying experience of her life. It had made clear to her the danger of such a journey, and the folly of her naivety.

Although, she forced herself to acknowledge, had she been traveling as a woman, it could have been much, much worse. As it was, it was bad enough. She was penniless and vulnerable and she had far to go.

Clearly, she needed a protector.

And this man? He would do well.

A pity he was so surly. As they rode, he was silent and any attempt at conversation was quashed by a scowl.

Which was fine. It gave her plenty of time to study him.

He was tall in the saddle, with strong thighs, and he rode with a military bearing she knew well. His face was raw and harsh, with sharp cheekbones and a straight blade of a nose, but his grey eyes softened his expression. They had a slumberous quality. It didn't hurt that his lashes were long and lacy.

The column of his neck was thick and there, traveling up and down the length of it, a manly knob. His chin, square and bold, was dusted with black bristles. His cheekbones were hard and high, his forehead broad. His shoulders were enormous, his chest massive. She imagined he was slabbed with muscle beneath his shirt. His lips were full, lush and beautifully formed. She could tell from the creases at the sides of them that he had smiled once, though he did not smile now.

Ah, but it was those eyes that arrested her the most, steely grey and steady, fringed by those incongruously lacy lashes. He was, in a word, beautiful.

But there was more to him than that. There was a familiarity. As though her soul saw and recognized his. She knew, knew beyond a shadow of a doubt, she was safe with him. He would protect her.

It was the way he carried himself, proud and humbled at the same time. The way he was steeped in a regimental honor. The tilt of his head. The ever-watching eyes.

She knew the look.

Graeme had had it.

This man would keep her safe…whether he wanted to or not.

Her heart told her she could trust him and after the debacle this journey had become, she needed someone she could trust. At the very least, she knew she couldn't travel all alone.

She decided to keep as close to him as she could. For safety. Nothing more than that, surely.

"What's your name, boy?"

His question, coming out of the blue as it did, after so much grumpy silence, startled her, but it took less than a second for her brain to come up with an answer. It was an easy one, the name Graeme used to call her when he tousled her hair or chucked her shoulder. "Pippin." She glanced at him when he did not respond. "And you are?"

There was no call for him to glower. But, at length, he responded with a grudging manner that made her wonder if his name was some national treasure, not to be easily given. "Daniel."

"It's nice to meet you, Daniel."

It was only the polite thing to say. There was no call for the sharp glance he shot her, as though her politesse annoyed him.

"So where are you traveling to, Pippin?" he asked after they'd gone a while in silence.

"Wick."

He made a grunting sound. "That is verra far indeed."

"Aye. It is." A long way to go with no money. At least the thief who had robbed her blind had not stolen her horse. She would be horribly lost then. Aside from which, Chelsea would be devastated.

"And where are you going?" she asked because it was the polite thing to do and because she was curious.

"Inverness." He said it in a slightly bitter tone that made her glance at him.

"Why are you going to Inverness?"

Something flickered through his eyes. She thought it might be annoyance, but it moved too quickly to be sure. "I have business there."

"What kind of business?"

Oh. Definitely annoyance. She was surprised to discover it was not aimed at her. For once.

"My uncle has perished."

"I'm so sorry."

"Don't be." His perfect face crumpled into a perfect moue. "He was a bastard. But, apparently, he has left me something and I have been summoned to his solicitor's office to collect it."

"What has he left you?" And what had this uncle done to deserve such vitriol?

"I doona know." He waved a hand and Fia couldn't help but wonder at the beauty of that appendage too. His hands were large, well-formed and strong. "Hence this folly of a journey across half of Britain. I doona know why they couldna ha' dropped a hint in the letter."

"Perhaps they worried you wouldna come if they told you."

His gaze pierced her and then, of all things, he barked a laugh. She liked the sound of it but judging from his expression, it surprised him. She had the sense he didn't laugh. Not as often as he might have liked.

"Why were you stealing apples?"

"I was hungry."

"There was an inn several miles back. You could have eaten there."

She looked away. No. She couldn't have eaten there. She didn't have a penny to her name.

"You doona have any money, do you, boy?"

She pressed her lips together.

"Do you no' realize how dangerous it is to travel with no money?"

"I was robbed."

"Robbed?"

"The blighter took all my coins and… everything I had."

He studied her a bit, then said, "And why are you going to Wick?"

Fia scrutinized him right back with equal diligence. "I am running away."

"Running away? From what?"

She set her chin. "A place I don't want to be."

"I see." From his tone, he probably did, although it was doubtful he could imagine the true circumstance. She had no intention of sharing that. "And you have people in Wick?"

Och. How to answer that? "Naturally." A lie always worked well.

Daniel frowned. It was clear the boy was lying. About something. If not everything.

It occurred to him the lad was far too young and far too naive to be traveling all alone. In the aftermath of the Peninsular War and the influx of destitute soldiers, the king's roads had become dangerous places to be when one was all alone. Daniel had rubbed up against some unsavory sorts on this journey, though no one had dared accost him. Probably on account of the saber tied to his saddle. If that didn't deter a villain, there was always the pistol he carried.

This boy was armed with nothing but...apples.

He didn't like the sense of protectiveness that arose within him. That worm in his brain that whispered he had some kind of obligation to protect this urchin. He did not. And he had no desire for a traveling companion.

He should simply tip his hat and say farewell to the boy before urging Hunnam into a gallop. He didn't know why he resisted.

It couldn't be that the boy reminded him of himself. He'd methodically expunged any memory of that helpless, vulnerable child. But if he was being truthful, this waif did remind him of someone else. Of Lennox. Something about the tip of his head, the slant of his eyes, the unruly mop of curls. And Lennox had had the same foolish enthusiasm in the face of adventure.

A trait that had gotten him killed.

How annoying it was that the two twined in his mind. That he entertained the thought that by protecting this boy he could somehow make amends for failing Lennox.

It was a ridiculous prospect.

He could never make amends for failing Lennox.

His soul wailed.

Well hell. This conversation needed to end and end now.

He set his teeth and put his heels to Hunnam's side. His mount charged forward.

To his annoyance, the mare followed.

CHAPTER FOUR

DANIEL LIFTED THE CHICKEN LEG AND TOOK A healthy bite. It was delicious. Savory. Rich and dripping with juice. He should enjoy it, but he couldn't.

The boy was watching him again and with a hungry expression Daniel found difficult to ignore. He resolved to ignore it.

There were many hungry boys in Scotland, no doubt. It was not *his* duty to feed them all.

Daniel turned to the left—angling his shoulder so the boy was behind him—and gazed out the window at the fields beyond the Clunie inn and focused his attention on the gamboling lambs. The hawk soaring by. A cloud. Aye, there were so many things to reflect upon, other than the hungry boy on the bench behind him.

Bedamned that he couldn't evict the urchin's face from his mind.

It was probably the fragility of his features that were so haunting, the sunken cheeks or the pleading eyes, or the slight tremble to the chin. The slender shoulders maybe.

He'd been a hungry boy once.

No one had fed him.

He glanced down at his plate, filled with potatoes and bread and chicken. He'd had a hearty breakfast today. He'd had apples. He had coin enough to pay for a soft bed to coddle his aching bones.

Did he really need this?

He glanced at the boy again, shivering by the fire, gaze skittering around the inn from one rowdy party to another, no doubt waiting for the innkeeper to shoo him away and back outside.

He remembered a boy seeking refuge in an inn one night when he had no money to pay. He remembered being sent away with an empty belly. He remembered the feeling of harboring such aloneness. Such fear.

All of a sudden, his appetite evaporated.

With a snarl, he stood and carried his plate over and thrust it at the boy.

That blue-green gaze skewered him. "Sir?" Hell. The child's voice hadn't even dropped yet.

"Go on," he snapped. "Eat it."

"Sir?" The boy's attention flickered to the plate. His tongue dashed out. He swallowed.

"Go on. Before I change my mind."

This time, the boy didn't hesitate. He grabbed the plate and stuffed the slab of bread in his mouth and rolled his eyes as though it were manna from heaven. "Thank you, sir," he mumbled through the food. "Thank you."

Daniel grunted and turned away, but that hard cold place in his chest warmed, just ever so slightly. The boy he had been was vindicated, if only a little. He lifted a finger at the innkeeper, silently ordering another meal. He was hungry after all. This one, he would probably eat in his rooms.

The next morning was just as beautiful as the previous days had been. Daniel headed out of the inn after a filling breakfast with the plan of making it to Moulin before sunset. That was probably a bit ambitious of him, but if he didn't make it, he wasn't above setting up camp beside the road and sleeping there. The innkeeper's wife had graciously packed him up a collation of food he could nibble on the way.

His steps stalled when he spotted the boy and the white mare waiting for him next to Hunnam in the stable yard.

He should have known better than to feed a stray.

And lord love a duck, he looked like a stray. Judging from the hay sprouting from his unruly curls, he'd slept in the stable loft. Judging from the smell clinging to his filthy clothes, he'd paid his way by mucking out the stalls.

It annoyed the hell out of Daniel that he *knew* this. He knew this because he'd once done the same.

That the boy was nibbling on an apple core—that had clearly been over-nibbled—while Daniel was suffering from an overfull belly after an obscenely decadent breakfast, didn't help. Guilt did not aid digestion. Nor did the outrage that came fist in glove with the certitude that said guilt was undeserved.

He owed the boy nothing. Nothing.

Fixing his features into a ferocious glower—so the pest would know better than to send any hungry looks in Daniel's direction—he heaved up into Hunnam's saddle. He set his teeth when the boy followed suit.

With a curse, Daniel flicked the reins and Hunnam charged forward.

It was a shame he hadn't been paying attention — or at least holding on better — because the lurch dethroned him. It wasn't the first time he'd lost his seat. Not the first time Hunnam, in his exuberance for a run, had tossed him into the dust. But it was probably one of the more humiliating times, on account of the fact that he'd been in the process of trying to appear superior and remote.

To his credit, the boy didn't laugh. Indeed, he hopped off his mare — with annoying ease — and offered Daniel a hand. It was a ridiculous prospect because Daniel was easily twelve stone and the boy was...a twig. The hand was slender and fragile. But it would have been churlish to refuse.

He allowed the boy to help him sit up, but no more than that. He needed some time, at any rate, to manage the blinding pain. It wasn't just the pain in his backside either. His leg sent up a hellish howl too. The mortification didn't help.

He shouldn't have had such a large breakfast. It threatened to come up. He found his hat and slapped it against his thigh to remove the worst of the dust and he glared at Hunnam, who pranced in the yard making sounds that sounded suspiciously like snickers.

At length, the agony subsided and he levered himself to his feet. He wanted to slap the boy's hands away, but the truth was, he appreciated the support. The last thing he wanted to do was tip over again.

Once he was steady, he whistled to Hunnam, who trotted over, still snorting his amusement. He shot the beast a glare and grabbed the reins. And then, because it was the polite thing to do, he nodded to the boy and said, "Thank you."

He did not say, "Please follow me for the rest of the day," but he might as well have. Because the boy did.

About two hours in, Daniel blew out a heavy breath and pulled up on Hunnam's reins. To his complete and utter aggravation, the boy stopped too. So he wheeled his mount and faced him head-on as such nuisances should be faced.

"Are you following me?" He attempted the query to be a bark, bold and bothered and befitting a formidable soldier of the Scots Greys.

Apparently, he'd lost his touch. His edge. His dire ferocity.

The boy grinned. It was a disarming grin with dimples and everything, and it did something to him, something deep inside him. Nudged at his soul. Urged it to awaken from its frozen slumber. It was a pity it was often cranky upon awakening. "Well? Are you?" Definitely cranky.

The irritating grin broadened. "In that I am behind you, yes. I suppose I'm following you." It annoyed him, that cheerful response. More than it should have. The voice that had not dropped. The trusting eyes. The smooth column of a neck that had no inkling how close it was to being throttled.

"Well, stop it."

The boy waved a hand at the guiltless road. "We're both traveling north it seems. It only makes sense to travel together."

Daniel's fingers tightened. "I prefer to travel alone." He deserved to travel alone.

"It would be safer to travel together." The mare shuffled closer, as though it were she who was frightened of the barren landscape surrounding them. Of the trees that could harbor any number of robbers. Of the hummocks that could, at any moment, rise up to trip them.

Without any urging on Daniel's part, Hunnam tossed his head and greeted the female of his species with a lascivious whinny.

Daniel yanked on the reins. Hunnam reared up, then rolled his eyes back and pinned Daniel with an equine glare. He entertained the very real prospect of being tossed again. This time on purpose. He shifted his annoyance to the boy, the boy who was far too trusting. "Where you came to the conclusion that I am a safe companion is a mystery." People who rode with him ended up dead. It was a known fact.

The boy blinked and Daniel was struck again at the clarity, the innocence of those eyes. "You fed me."

As simple as that.

As devastatingly simple as that.

He should never have weakened. He should never have shown any mercy.

God protect him from tender emotions. And hungry boys.

"Why did you choose *me* to torment?" Of all the travelers on the road, how had *he* been the lucky one?

A slender shoulder rose. "You remind me of my brother."

Hell. "How so?" However so?

"You're a military man."

"I most certainly am not."

"You were." A simple, incontrovertible truth. "I can trust you." And that, a folly.

"I am no' a man to be trusted."

"You *fed* me." Did he need to harp on that one failing so?

With a grumble that sounded suspiciously like a snarl, Daniel urged Hunnam forward. His shadow hurried to catch up.

They rode in silence. It was pleasant. It was nice. It was quiet. He had no idea why suddenly, out of the blue, he opened his mouth and spoiled it. "So you come from a military family?"

Surely he didn't care. Surely he didn't want to know more about this sad, vulnerable urchin.

The boy bobbed his head. "Aye."

Daniel studied his person. Smallish for a soldier, still, he asked, "Do you intend to enlist? When you're grown?"

The boy's lips curved, some secret jest. "The war is over," he said.

"There will be other wars." Probably. Just not for Daniel. He was ruined for military service. Forever. And what else did he have? Who the hell else was he? *What* was he?

A groom? For the remainder of his life?

"I think no'." A slender shoulder lifted. "I doona fancy myself of the disposition to kill."

"It comes more easily than you could imagine." Flesh separated like warm butter. Blood flowed. Men fell. And after a while, one could forget what the fall of a saber would mean to the poor sod on the other end of it. One could forget that they were men. That they had wives and mothers and children. That they had lived well, up until now.

One could even justify it with a well-worn lie. Something like, *It is either him or me.*

War was full of well-worn lies.

Far too late, Daniel discovered he too was not of the disposition to kill. He never wanted to kill another thing. Not ever again.

He found his thoughts, his memories, his horrors discomfiting. Maybe that was why he extended a conversation he had not wanted in the first place. "Was your father in the service?"

He shook his head. "My brother."

"Your brother is military?"

The lad glanced away. "Was. He…died."

"I see." Occupational hazard.

"In Belgium."

Daniel's heart skipped a painful beat. "Belgium?" So many had. Lost their lives there. "He fought at Waterloo?"

A sigh. "That's what the letter said."

Ah. The letter. Daniel had written his share. He hated those damned letters.

"I'm sorry for your loss." It was a patent pleasantry. And an empty one. And the words hurt like hell. Like gravel in his throat.

Large eyes lifted to meet his. He ignored the welling dampness. Dampness was irrelevant. "He was my only family. He was all I had."

Hell. Why did he suddenly feel responsible for this boy? This lad? This child? Had he written the letter that had changed Pippin's life? Did it matter if he had or not?

Hell.

Hell and damnation.

Enough of this. He didn't want to travel with someone. Traveling with someone made him responsible for their safety and he did not want the onus. He couldn't carry any more guilt. And staring down at that woebegone face made something inside him lurch, twist in an aching way.

No. He did not want a traveling companion. And certainly not this one.

He flicked the reins with more vigor than was necessary and Hunnam bounded forward. When the boy followed suit, annoyance prickled at Daniel's nape. "Must you follow so close?"

The boy blinked. "We are travelling together."

"We most certainly are not." He ignored the flicker of pain that flashed over that woebegone face, and pressed on. "I told you. I prefer to travel alone. I doona want conversation. I doona want companionship. And I certainly doona want to *feed* you." The boy's mouth opened, most probably to issue some irritating rebuttal, but Daniel didn't allow it. "For God's sake, leave me alone, boy," he said in a feral growl. "You are a nuisance." And then he gored Hunnam in the flanks and pounded down the north road, leaving the guttersnipe in his dust.

Well, Fia sniffed as she watched the great grey disappear around a curve. *That was rude.*

But then, hadn't she expected as much?

Her soldier had been nothing but surly from the start. He'd made no secret of the fact he didn't want her companionship.

Fine. Just fine. If he didn't want her to travel with him, she wouldn't. She tried not to be discouraged at the thought. Despite his grumbly attitude, she'd enjoyed his company — or his presence at the very least, as he hadn't been terribly companionable. And for some reason, she'd liked him.

She urged Blaze to catch up, but she was careful to make sure she stayed out of his sight. He stopped for lunch at the inn in Ballinluig and Fia stopped as well, to rest her mount. As Blaze drank from the River Tummel, Fia leaned against a tree stump and ate an apple.

She loved apples, but they did become tiring when one ate nothing else. She'd shown great restraint last night when Daniel had handed her his plate. She'd eaten only half and then carefully wrapped up the bread and some of the chicken for later. She had no idea when she would have the opportunity to eat again. Some of the innkeepers were happy to give her chores in exchange for a spot of food and a place to sleep, but many others were irritable and annoyed at the request. Beyond that, between Moulin and Newtonmore, there were not many inns.

Hopefully, there would be plenty of orchards.

She leaned back and closed her eyes and let the heat of the sun warm her skin. She hadn't slept well the night before. The hay had been scratchy and since being robbed, she hadn't been able to fully relax. Every noise had awakened her. Her muscles ached from mucking out the stables in Clunie and her stomach was empty—apples notwithstanding.

She hadn't expected traveling to be so exhausting. It discouraged her to think how far there was yet to go. And apparently, she would be making the journey alone. It would have been so nice to have a companion.

When Daniel didn't emerge from the inn for some time, she sighed and gathered her reins, mounted Blaze and continued on the north road.

She tried to ignore the trickle of trepidation, twined as it was with a deep, abiding disappointment.

He did not want her company. She wouldn't force it upon him.

The boy had stopped following him. Finally.

Or perhaps he'd taken the crossroads at Ballinluig. Each time Daniel glanced over his shoulder, there was not so much as a hint of him.

Something curled in his belly. He'd become used to that occasional flash of white when he peeked over his shoulder. It had amused him. More than it should have. And, if he were being honest, it had soothed him a little to know he wasn't utterly alone on this road.

But now the boy was gone.

It was foolish to miss him.

Daniel had told him, in no uncertain terms, that he was a nuisance—

Heat crept up his neck. Had he? Had he really?

What kind of man did that? What kind of honorable man saw someone in need and ignored him? Nay, rebuffed him. Granted, there was something about the boy that poked at a festering wound in his soul. His vulnerability, his trust, his resemblance to Daniel's closest friend, now dead. But that was no excuse for Daniel's behavior. His mother would have been mortified. Indeed, she was probably looking down on him from heaven and shaking her head, as she had done when he was young and foolish and thoughtless. She would expect better of him. And he should expect better of himself.

He was tempted to turn around and ride back to the inn, to find the boy and feed him again. And he would have, if he hadn't acquired another traveling companion at the Ballinluig inn.

Ennis Campbell had sat next to Daniel at the rough table and struck up a conversation. He'd been pleased to discover the man had served with the Inniskillings Dragoons and in that, they had much in common. They were also both traveling north. It only made sense to travel together.

After a congenial chat and a satisfying meal, they set out together on the road to Moulin. It occurred to Daniel, as they drank and talked, that he'd been solitary for far too long. It was rejuvenating indeed to laugh and joke with others, to remember what it was like to be alive. What it was to be well.

He wasn't sure why it was so healing, this traveling, but it was. Maybe because it gave him things to think about other than how much his spirit ached. It wasn't that he hadn't thought of Lennox all day, he had. His friend was rarely far from his mind. The guilt of his death was never absent from Daniel's heart. But the opportunity to help someone else, as he had helped that boy, though in very small ways, did ease the sting.

Could it be that was the secret to dealing with unbearable pain — finding small ways to ease it in others?

He should have invited the boy into the inn. He should have fed him again. Daniel hadn't missed the sight of him leaning against the stump by the river...eating a damn apple. How easy would it have been to wave him over? Invite him in?

Yet he hadn't.

Now he was having second thoughts. Regret for losing what had been a tolerable companion. Guilt for being so irascible, for certain, but there was more. For failing the boy. Just as he had failed Lennox.

It didn't help that he and Ennis passed from the open road surrounded by fields into an apple orchard. As they rode through the fragrant shadowed road, desire rose within him, and not just for apples. Desire, perhaps, to be a better man.

It was probably too late for that, but he couldn't evict the thought.

Daniel's attention stalled, mid-regret, as he caught a flash of white through the trees. His heart skipped. His mood rose.

Was it...? Could it be...?

Ah yes. It was.

A white mare.

He slowed his mount to scan the orchard and Ennis slowed beside him.

Blast. He didn't see the boy. Where was he? Had his horse thrown him? Was he wounded? Lying on the ground broken and bloodied? Heat rose on his neck. God, he hoped not.

His companion cleared his throat, capturing Daniel's attention.

And then something else captured his attention. Something that caused his pulse to skitter, his muscles to lock.

The smile, certainly, with which Ennis presented him. It was cold and reptilian at best. But it was the pistol, pointed at Daniel's chest, that absorbed him. He'd stared down the barrel of a pistol before.

He did not care for the sensation.

He also did not care to be robbed.

"Get off the horse."

Daniel gaped at him. Ennis intended to steal his horse? Hunnam? His friend? The charger that had kept him alive on a French battlefield when men were falling around him like flies?

Hell no.

He growled in response. His fury blossomed. The soldier within him arose and he unsheathed his saber with a singing hiss. A pity his pistol was in his bag, or he would have reached for that.

Ennis chuckled and eased his mount back, out of reach of the blade. "I have a pistol," he said, by way of a mocking reminder.

Did he have any idea? Any clue how quickly Daniel could charge? He was a cavalryman. He'd killed before. And any man who thought to steal his horse deserved to die.

"Come now, Sinclair," Ennis said cheerfully. "Get off the horse. I will shoot you to have him."

"Do you know what they do to horse thieves?" he snapped. They hung them. That was what they did. Ennis would be lucky to live that long.

"Aye. I do. But they'll never catch me." He grinned. "They never have yet. Now. If you please." He waggled the pistol. "Dismount."

Anger, frustration and a hint of panic skirled through Daniel's soul. He couldn't allow this man to have Hunnam. He knew he could charge but a bullet would travel much faster than a horse. Besides which, he couldn't take the chance of Hunnam being shot.

The best thing to do was to engage in the pretense of giving over his horse...and then, if he could, retrieve his own pistol. If Ennis took off with Hunnam, Daniel could always whistle him back.

His mount was exquisitely trained.

Daniel prepared to dismount, but before he could, a round, red missile whizzed past his head and smacked into the weapon. The impact caused Ennis to squeeze the trigger and the pistol fired into the trees. The retort was deafening in the peaceful calm of the afternoon, but not so deafening that Daniel didn't hear a high-pitched cry.

His heart stilled, because he was certain he recognized that voice.

He turned to the trees just as another missile whizzed through the air. It hit Ennis in the back of the head with a dull thud. The man whirled around and yet another connected with his forehead. This one shattered, leaving a wet white goo in his hair. Suddenly, Daniel realized what the missiles were. Not rocks. Apples. And they continued to fly.

Ennis valiantly tried to fend off the attack, waving his arms before him, but the apples flew fast and furious.

While his assailant was thusly preoccupied, Daniel fished out his pistol and trained it on the brigand. When Ennis noticed it, his features clenched and his gaze danced up the road, toward escape. Without hesitation, he hunched over his mount and took off, back the way they'd come.

Daniel was of a mind to follow him—to follow him and capture him, tie him hand and foot and drag him to the constable in Moulin—but he was forestalled in this when, to his left, a familiar form dropped from the leafy branches of an apple tree.

He couldn't stop his grin at the sight of the boy, his erstwhile companion. And then his breath locked.

A red bloom stained the sleeve of the urchin's shirt.

He'd been shot.

CHAPTER FIVE

*W*ELL, HELL.

Fia clutched at her arm where a wayward bullet had grazed her shoulder.

Bullets *hurt*.

She'd never expected there to be so much blood.

To be precise, she'd never expected to be shot. But when she'd seen that horrible man pull a gun on Daniel and demand that he dismount, she'd been filled with a righteous fury. Not only because she knew the horror of being robbed of the one thing you loved more than anything—and it was clear Daniel loved his horse. Not only because thieves were, at their very core, reprehensible and deserved, above all things, to be splatted with apples. And not just because she had *liked* him.

There was more to it, that feeling of protectiveness that had risen up, that sense of allegiance. But she couldn't put a name to the feeling.

She'd never felt it before.

"Holy God. Are you all right?"

Daniel threw himself from his stallion's back and rushed to her side.

Fia flinched as he neared. Covering her wound, she turned away. "I'm fine. It's nothing."

His brows lowered. "It's not nothing. Let me see."

Oh God. No! She couldn't let him see! To do so, she would have to remove her shirt. And that would be a disaster. "I'm fine."

"Damn it, boy. Let me have a look."

"It's nothing." *Oh heavens.* She tried to walk away, but for some reason, her legs wouldn't carry her. Her head spun and her mouth went dry. Prickles danced down her arm. She stumbled and then collapsed and by the grace of God, he caught her. His hold was strong and warm and comforting.

And his scent? What was that? A woodsy loam and a hint of manly musk? She'd never smelled the like.

She tried to make her mind focus, but the thoughts kept dancing away.

Gently, he leaned her against the tree and reached for the buttons of her shirt. She had to stop him. He couldn't know. No one could know. She set her hand on his and looked up into his beautiful grey eyes, so full of care and concern. It was tempting to allow herself to be cared for again.

"No." A croak. "Please."

His lips firmed. And they were such fine and beautiful lips. They captured her attention and made her feel quite woozy. She was possessed of a sudden urge to taste them, although she didn't know why.

"Pippin. I must check your wound. And what were you thinking anyway? Barraging him with apples? The man was holding a gun."

A trickle of manic humor whipped through her. "I was thinking I wouldn't be shot."

"Good God," he grumbled. "You need a keeper." He renewed his attempt to unbutton her shirt until she captured both his hands.

"I do," she giggled. She had no idea why he scowled. "At least he dinna get your horse."

Daniel blew out a breath. "He would never have had my horse. But aside from that, it wasna worth you risking your life."

She attempted to focus on him although, as the dark cloud descended, he became somewhat blurry. "I doona like thieves."

"Nor do I, but you shouldna ha' risked your life as you did."

"Pish."

He reared back. "Did you say *pish*?"

"I did." She grinned. "I was completely hidden in the branches."

"He still managed to hit you."

"That was a fluke."

"He had a *loaded* gun. He could have hit anything. You're lucky you are not dead."

"Pish." There was nothing else to say. Besides which, her brain was becoming fuzzier and it was harder to think. The pain in her arm was still sharp but was becoming a warm glow. And my, he was diligent in his attempts to disrobe her, despite her diligent efforts to stop him.

It devolved into something of a scuffle.

"Pippin, I must see. I need to stop the bleeding. I need to know if the bullet is still in your arm."

It wasn't. She knew it. It had only grazed her, but she couldn't form the words. A great fatigue closed in on her like a rolling fog. Her lids became too heavy to hold open. "Daniel?" A wraith of a whisper.

"Aye, Pippin?"

"Do be gentle."

He made a sound. Something strangled. "Gentle? I...of course."

"And Daniel?"

He sighed. "Aye, Pippin?"

"Do forgive me."

"Forgive you?" Did she imagine the thread of tenderness in his tone? "For what, lad?"

She rallied her strength. She had to tell him. He needed to know. He would discover for himself, and soon. Indeed, even now, she could feel the lapels of her rough shirt loosening. But for some reason she very much wanted him to hear it from her own lips.

"For what, lad?" he prompted.

"For lying to you."

Lying?

About what?

Daniel gazed down at the boy, his mind awhirl. For one thing, he was concerned about the lad's color. He'd gone a disturbing grey. His delicate features, which had been far too pronounced before, were positively sunken. That he could barely speak, that his mind was clearly wandering were also bad signs.

But what on earth had he lied about? Hell, they'd barely had a complete conversation.

It hardly mattered though. Daniel knew from past experience, this wound needed to be treated. If nothing else, the boy was going into shock. Once his hands fell away, Daniel deftly unbuttoned his shirt and tugged the shoulder down. The lesion was deep, but not serious. The bullet had, indeed, glanced him, which was lucky. But he'd lost a lot of blood and he was still bleeding. The injury needed to be cleaned and bound.

Daniel pushed back, intent on heading for his saddlebags for the necessary items, when something captured his attention and he stilled.

Froze.

Stared.

Holy hell.

He didn't know much in this world, but he surely recognized a breast when he saw one. A perfect, lush breast with a delicate coral tip.

After a stunned moment of study, his gaze flicked to that face once more. Those elegant, fragile lines. The high cheekbones, the slender nose, the swanlike neck, the bow-shaped lips and almond-shaped eyes with a thick shadow of lashes.

Hell.

How had he not seen it?

How had he not known?

For not only was she decidedly female, she was exquisite. The sight of her, the knowledge of her, awoke something within him. A burn. A want. A hunger he barely recognized, an urge he could no longer name. It wasn't lust. It couldn't be.

But it was something.

The desire to feel again, perhaps.

Though he was in a daze, he lurched up and riffled in the saddlebags. He had no idea how he found what he needed. No idea how he cleaned the wound and wrapped it. No idea how he found another shirt for her — one of his, which was way too large, but at least it wasn't soaked in blood.

His mind was utterly beset with the realization that this lad — this lad he had deserted, more than once, left to his own devices in a dangerous, treacherous world — was no boy at all.

Guilt rose again to claim him but he didn't allow it. He was beyond that. What was done was done. What mattered now was keeping this woman safe. That, and the choices he made moving forward.

Though it was only early afternoon, he knew they wouldn't be traveling any farther today so he went about setting up camp, building a fire and making a comfortable pallet for her. Oh, it wasn't as comfortable as a bed in an inn, but it would do. For his part, he could sleep anywhere.

After that he tended to the horses—hers and his—and then prepared a meal for when she awakened.

And then, when all of that was done, he sat with his back against a tree and watched her sleep.

He shouldn't have. He knew he shouldn't have, but he couldn't help it. There was something about her that drew his gaze, captured it, held it. He thought back to their earlier interactions—attempting not to cringe as he remembered how horrid he'd been. He focused instead on all she'd said, her tone, the timbre of her voice.

She'd been robbed.

She was hungry.

She was traveling all alone.

And then, when he'd asked why she was going to Wick: *I am running away.* From a place she did not want to be.

Holy God. How could he not have responded to that? Asked more? He could only imagine what had happened. And his imaginings devastated him.

He'd asked her then if she had people in Wick and she had hesitated.

He set his teeth. When she awoke, he had questions for her. And by God, she would answer.

When Fia came to, it was dusk. She knew at once she was still in the apple orchard where she'd been shot—*shot!*—

but she was alone. A flare of panic rose until she saw the huge grey stallion hobbled next to Blaze, and Daniel's saddlebags propped against a tree.

Thank God. He hadn't left her.

She sat up and winced as pain danced down her arm. She glanced at it and was surprised to see she wore a clean shirt, though it was huge on her. The neckline draped down over her shoulder, exposing a good portion of her chest. Heat prickled and she rearranged the garment.

Holy heaven. He knew. He *knew*.

What was more, he'd *seen* her.

He had to have, if he bound her wound. If he changed her clothes.

He knew.

A movement to her right captured her attention. Daniel emerged from the falling shadows, carrying a bucket in one hand. When he noticed her gaze on him, he stilled. His lips tightened.

Oh dear.

But he came to kneel by her, handing her a cup of water. "How are you feeling?" he asked.

She took the cup and drank greedily, then said on a damp gust, "Fine. Better." She couldn't hold his gaze. "I…ah, thank you for helping me."

He barked a laugh, which made her glance at him. She was surprised to see his lips tweak into a smile. "Thank you for helping *me*." He settled beside her and dipped the cup in the bucket once more. "I dinna say it earlier, but I do appreciate what you did."

"You did appear to need saving."

For some reason, he scowled. "I dinna. But I thank you nonetheless. It was verra brave."

His words made her want to puff out her chest. It wasn't often she felt brave, but it was nice to be considered as such.

A pity he went and ruined it by adding, "But foolish."

"Foolish?"

"You really must restrain yourself in future, Pippin." His eyes narrowed. "If that is indeed your name."

Indeed, it was not. But she didn't respond; annoyance with him prickled at her nape and she set her teeth, glaring at him mutinously.

He blew out a breath. "Did you think I wouldna notice?"

"Notice?" She fluttered her lashes as innocently as she could.

He didn't appreciate her dissembling. His brow lowered into something that could have been terribly ominous if he hadn't been so damned handsome. And so close. If he didn't smell so...delicious. "That you are a woman." A whisper. If that.

"Ah." She took another sip. "You wouldna ha' noticed, had I not been shot." This she said with all the aplomb she could muster. "My disguise was verra good."

He snorted. "How could anyone be fooled?"

"*You* were fooled."

"I most certainly was not."

"Pish."

He waggled a finger at her. "See. That. Just there. Boys doona say pish."

"Pish."

"And that..." He waved a hand at her face.

"That what?"

"Your..."

"My what?"

"Your face. Your nose. Your eyes. Your lips. Those lashes."

She fluttered them once more. "I do have them."

"No boy has such fine features."

Had he called her fine? Well, this was going nicely. She had no idea why he looked so exasperated.

He sat back and fixed her with a brooding frown, which she attempted to ignore. Daintily, she slurped her water and fixed her attention on the road instead.

"You should ha' told me you were a woman," he said. "I would no' have deserted you."

"I'm gratified to know that."

"Damn it, Pippin! Do you have any idea how dangerous these roads can be?"

She lifted her arm. "I *am* shot."

He glared. "For a woman. You could have been…accosted."

"I *was* robbed."

"You know what I mean. There are worse things. I would never have forgiven myself if…"

"Ah, but you would never have known."

For some reason, he didn't find this logic soothing. "From here on out, we are traveling together." This, he barked. A command.

She hardly minded the idea, but the bossy bits of it set her teeth on edge. Which was probably why she murmured, quite beneath her breath, "I believe I suggested that."

He paled. His lips worked. An agonized expression flickered through his eyes.

She swept away the guilt at causing his chagrin. Because it was true. She *had* suggested it. But his only response was a muttered, "We are traveling together."

Her stomach growled and she set her hand to it. She took another sip of water to help ease the pang. Daniel's expression darkened. He leaped to his feet. "Oh my God. You havena had anything to eat."

Not true in the slightest. "I've had apples." Plenty of apples. She'd eaten several perched up there in the tree—surely not waiting for him to pass by.

He shot her another pained glance. "I have pork pie."

Another growl, nay a howl. She swallowed the drool in her mouth. "P-pork pie?"

"Aye." He riffled in his bags and pulled out a small wrapped package. He thrust it at her. "Here."

"I canna eat your pie."

"You must. You've been wounded." He forced a grin and swept out his arm to encompass the orchard. "I shall have apples."

"We shall share." She unwrapped the pasty and broke it in half before he could demur. When he took his half, their fingers brushed. It sent a skein of heat down her spine.

The taste, the delicious explosion of flavor on her tongue, filled her with warmth and utter satisfaction. She'd been so hungry. And this, this was bliss.

Daniel settled down beside her, which made her feel very warm as well. She was certain it was only that she was pleased not to be alone. Surely it had nothing to do with the fact that he was a man. A large, looming, handsome man. Who was warm and generous and wanted to protect her. And *feed* her.

She shot a look at him as he licked some juice from his slender fingers and her gaze stalled. My. His fingers were long, his hands large. His forearms muscled and sprinkled with fascinating black hairs. And his chest, so broad. His shoulders were massive. They rather made her breath catch. And then there was his neck...thick and sturdy. She liked his chin. Square and strong with the hint of a dent. And his lips of course. She had already studied those at length. His nose was fine too, noble and strong. And his eyes...

She stalled at his eyes, those somber grey orbs fringed with thick lashes...because they were fixed on her.

Oh dear.

He'd caught her staring.

But he didn't frown or wince or anything quite so heinous. Instead, he swallowed. She tracked his Adam's apple as it made the leisurely slide down and then up the column of his throat.

She met his gaze again and something shot through her, something unfamiliar and at the same time as recognizable as her own name. It felt like hunger, but a hunger of the soul.

She wanted nothing more than to kiss him.

It was a silly urge. Surely a man like this would want nothing to do with a woman like her. For one thing, she was dressed as a boy. For another, she was penniless and helpless and bleeding.

Aye, it was a silly urge, but one difficult to thrust away.

On her endless journey to who-knew-what, she'd had a lot of time to think about what the future might hold. She knew it wouldn't be the one she had envisioned growing up.

She'd always dreamed of finding love, experiencing passion, belonging to someone. All that had been stripped from her upon Graeme's death. Now, there would be no season. There would be no titled husband. No husband whatsoever. There would be no suitors—for who wanted a penniless servant? Everything she'd ever envisioned for herself had dried up and blown away one summer's day in Belgium. And while she couldn't deny deep regret at the loss of a life that should have been hers, in truth, it wasn't the money, houses or titles she would miss as much as the choices such privilege had afforded her, the ability to frame her own world.

Her choices were limited now.

But suddenly, as she stared into Daniel's eyes, she saw something else. Another possibility dawned.

She *did* have choices.

They were just...different choices.

She could know passion, if she chose.

And if she did, if she could choose, she would choose a man like this.

She toyed with the fabric of her sleeve. It suddenly occurred to her that this had to be his shirt. She wasn't sure why the thought sent a skitter of delight through her.

It was probably for the best that he wrenched his gaze away just then, or she might have made a fool of herself. She had been mooning. A little.

She didn't miss the rise of a flush on his cheeks, although it could have been a trick of the fire.

"So." He glanced around the clearing, searching for a change of topic, no doubt. "You said your brother was in the military?"

"Aye."

"Lost at Waterloo?"

"Aye."

She thought he might ask more, but he didn't. His lips tightened and he turned his attention to the fire. His expression took on the flicker of flames and Fia had the sense he was living it all again.

It pained her that he was suffering it alone. That was probably why she said, "Would you tell me about it?" Though, if she were being truthful, there was another reason she asked. A far more selfish one.

"Tell you about...what?" he asked, but she could tell, from the bunching of the muscle in his cheek, he knew what she meant.

She scooted closer and said softly, "Tell be about the battle. Tell me about Waterloo."

CHAPTER SIX

DANIEL'S GUT CLENCHED. HE DIDN'T WANT TO TALK about it. He didn't want to think about it. He wanted to close his eyes and have all memory of it waft away. Would that it could. Aside from which, her tender ears didn't deserve such abuse as an accounting of the worst day of his life. So he was brief. "It was a battle. Bloody. Brutal. Many died." Too many. "Nothing more to say."

"Please?" Her voice caught. "I want to know what my brother knew. I want to know how he died."

Nae, young lass. You doona.

It occurred to him that he should ask the question coiling in his mind. He should ask her brother's name. But he didn't. He couldn't.

What if he'd known him? What if he'd watched him die? What if her brother was one of the men he didn't save? Nae. It was far too painful to consider. Far too raw to even ask.

"Tell me *something.*"

Good lord. How on earth could he refuse her that? Her eyes were so beseeching. Her expression devastated him.

He steeled his spine. Drew in a deep breath. "It rained." Rained like hell the day before and most of the night. The ground was soft and sucking, the mud nearly impassable. Even the horses struggled in some places.

Pippin put out a lip. "Everyone knows that. Tell me something else." She settled back as though preparing for a bedtime story. *Hell*. Daniel should tell her everything. The cries, the random body parts, the blood. So much of it. But if he did, she would never fall asleep. She might never sleep again. When his hesitation became too long, she prompted, "Tell me about the Greys."

Ah. The Greys. The love of his life. His purpose. His meaning…until he was of use to them no more.

"Were you an officer?"

Daniel snorted. "I was no'. I couldna afford a commission." Hell, he could barely afford a horse. If it hadn't been for James Hamilton's sponsorship, he couldn't have. But for some reason, Hamilton—a major when Daniel had arrived in Redford Barracks as a young boy with dreams of fighting for the Royal Dragoons—had seen something in him. Hamilton had taken him under his wing. Been his mentor, his friend, his commanding officer.

It had been hell, watching him die.

Hamilton was far from the first man Daniel would see die on a bloody field that day, but his death was, by far, one of the most difficult to witness. Hamilton had been leading the charge as they plowed into a line of French infantry, with Daniel not far behind.

Too far behind.

Too far to stop a French lancer from taking Hamilton's arm. Undaunted, Daniel's hero had gripped the reins between his teeth and forged onward, fighting for the right and might of the cause. Fighting to defeat the monster Napoleon had become. Hamilton was a man nothing could stop. Until a bullet did. Right in the heart. It had been quick. One moment he was there, dirty and determined and filled with the unquenchable fury of battle...and the next, he was gone.

"Daniel?" Her voice was soft, soothing. It brought him back from the maw of hell, saved him from the dark memory that threatened to consume him whole. It was a blessing.

"What...what would you like to know?"

She lifted her uninjured shoulder. "Anything. Anything would...help."

Ah God. Yes. He knew the feeling. The hunger for something, anything, to connect with someone who had disappeared one summer day on a bloody field never to be seen again...

It would take some effort, but he would tell her what he could. She was the sister of one of his fallen comrades; he owed her at least that much. He sucked in a deep breath and began.

"We arrived in Brussels on the 15th of June. There were six troops in our regiment, under the command of James Hamilton."

"Ah." She nodded. "I know his name."

The admiration in her gaze warmed him, urged him on. "Aye and Hamilton was under Wellington's command."

"I know his name too."

Daniel's lips quirked. "Everyone does." Everyone should. "Ponsonby was in command of the brigade. The Royal Dragoons, Inniskillings Dragoons and the Scots Greys."

"And did you fight in the Battle of Quatre Bras?"

He shook his head, trying not to grimace. "We missed that one. And we nearly missed Waterloo too." Would that they had. "The trek was arduous. I did mention it was raining?"

"You did."

"When we arrived, the battle had already begun. Command decided to hold us back in reserve. But then...things werena going well and Hamilton ordered us forward. Ach, we were chomping at the bit by then. It was difficult knowing other men were fighting and dying while we *waited*." He could remember it, that feeling of blinding, seething frustration. The smells of scorched fields, the sound of the distant cannons, the great clouds of smoke filling the sky, barely dampened by the incessant drizzle of rain.

He must have drifted off, back into memory, for she nudged him. He hadn't realized she'd moved so close, but somehow, he liked her closeness. Needed it. "Hamilton ordered you forward?"

Ah yes. When the order came to attack, they'd leapt into action. They'd flown into the fray without hesitation. "We were ordered to attack the third division of the French army. They'd been pummeling our lines and our orders were to break them. It was difficult going at first. The fields were uneven and wet. But we picked up speed as we approached." He paused and gazed out into the shadows of night, reliving that glorious ride. It was the last he would have for a long while.

"Did you break the lines?"

He snorted a laugh, though it held little humor. "Imagine, if you will, a field of soldiers on their feet, attempting to fend off an onrushing tide of that." He waved to Hunnam. Muscled, strong. Invincible.

They had been. They'd sliced through the French ranks as though they were made of sticks.

"Once we broke their lines, they didn't stand a chance. We swept through them like a raging storm."

"It sounds magnificent."

It had been hellish, but he couldn't tell her that. Couldn't mention the blood, the bodies, the destruction. He scrubbed his face. "We defeated the column and one of our men captured the French Eagle."

"Ewart."

"Aye." Another name everyone knew.

"We should have retreated then, those were our orders, but the fighting was intense and blood was high. After that advance, we turned toward the French artillery." It had been then that the battle had become true chaos. Orders were lost and misunderstood. Confusion reigned. They'd ridden directly into the French infantry fire and lost...so many men. Including Hamilton.

Daniel could still see him fall, the look of surprise in his eyes.

But they hadn't stopped. At that point, they couldn't. To stop was to die.

"We found ourselves surrounded by the enemy. The French cavalry swept down on us. Ponsonby was captured. Well, hell, he was our brigade commander. We werena having any of that." And damn. That was the heart of his story, wasn't it? The aching, bleeding heart.

For as hard as it had been to watch Hamilton die, it didn't hold a candle to his agony over losing Lennox. In Daniel's zeal to rescue Ponsonby, he hadn't noticed the boy was following him. By the time he realized the danger, it was too late. The lancers had rushed their position, goring Scots at will.

"I watched my friend die there." Wispy words, threaded with a prickly ribbon of guilt. For though he hadn't cut down Lennox himself, he was no more innocent in his friend's death. If only he'd kept his eye on the boy in the melee. If only he hadn't been so enthusiastic about the advance. He should have protected him better.

Lennox was too young, too inexperienced, too enthusiastic by far.

"It was my fault he died." The hardest words he ever put to lip. He'd never told anyone.

"How so?"

"I should ha' protected him."

"I imagine it was pandemonium."

"Aye. It was."

She set her hand on his. It was warm. The heat soaked in and filled him somehow. "You canna protect everyone. Especially not in the confusion of battle." True. But it was his obligation to try. "And he joined the fray of his own accord." Again true. "You canna take responsibility for his actions, Daniel. You canna."

He stared at her. Something in him shifted, lightened, lifted. He wasn't sure what it was, but it felt…nice.

"What happened to Ponsonby?"

"They killed him. Stabbed him in the heart." And Lennox with him. And many more.

They'd nearly killed Daniel as well. As it was, they'd nearly won his leg. He'd taken a lance to the thigh—far too close to his groin to leave him a man—but even with that, he'd been one of the lucky ones. He'd survived.

Despite the agony of a French blade in his thigh, despite the screaming horror in his soul at the loss of his mentor and of his friend, he continued to fight.

Oh, not for the right and might of Britain. Not for the lives of his fellow soldiers. To his chagrin, to his utter mortification and unending guilt, he had fought for his life.

To survive. Nothing more. Certainly nothing that looked or smelled or tasted of honor.

Some could say they had run. Turned tail and fled the much superior French numbers. But if they hadn't retreated, they would have died. Each and every one of them. Upon reflection, it might have been best.

"We lost one hundred and four men that day. Two hundred and twenty-eight horses."

"But you survived."

"Aye. I survived." Daniel turned his attention to the fire, somehow seeing the red of the battlefield that day licking through the flames. Each crack the retort of a rifle, each hiss the wail of the dying. "We attended a ball, you know. Just a few nights before the battle."

Her expression had gone soothing, as though she could see Daniel's torment and wanted to ease it. There was no easing it. "I've never been to a ball."

"Neither had I. I certainly never expected I would be at one." His laugh was harsh, but still a laugh. "I imagine I looked as frightened as I felt." In some ways, the ball had been more terrifying than the battle itself. Perhaps that was why he mentioned it. Or perhaps he had mentioned it to wipe clean the memories of the horrors that followed. Retreat to a simpler time when all he had to worry about was spilling his drink on a costly carpet or making a *faux pas* in the presence of England's elite. Lords, ladies, barristers, landowners and the military's highest leaders had attended the Duchess of Richmond's ball. He'd probably stood out like a sore Scots thumb.

"Why did you go?"

"Why?" Why did anyone accept an invitation from a friend on the eve of a war? "I was told there would be excellent food."

"Was there?"

He thought back. It took a moment. "I suppose there was." But it was more than that now, that night. It was the last time he and Lennox had laughed together. The last time they'd shared a drink. The last time they'd snuck off—into Richmond's library, on this occasion—for a game of chess.

"Did you dance with a lady?"

The question startled him from his musings. "I most certainly did not." He tipped his head and shot her a chagrined look. "I doona know how to dance. It would have exposed me for the poser I was. But the Gordons danced reels."

"That must have been a sight to see."

"Indeed. Unfortunately, news came while we were at that ball, that Napoleon was advancing and…" The evening had not ended well.

Pippin sighed. "I always thought it would be wonderful to attend a ball."

He glanced at her and, of a sudden, he *saw* her. Not as he assumed her to be, but as she was. A girl who had lost everything, even something as simple as the chance at a ball. And he realized, not only the soldiers of Waterloo had sacrificed. Families had. The country had. The world.

One of their earlier conversations filled his mind and curiosity nudged him. "Why were you running away?"

She jumped as though his question surprised her. "What?"

"The day we met, when I asked why you were going to Wick, you said you were running away. From a place you dinna want to be."

Her face crumpled into an annoyed moue. It was adorable. "You certainly have a good memory."

"I do. I'm also relentless when I want answers." She didn't respond, which incited him to ask again. "So… Why were you running away?"

A shoulder lifted. The shirt she wore—his shirt—slipped down, revealing a tantalizing expanse of skin, a hint of a curve. It sent an inconvenient and pointless yearning through him. The desire to mold his hand around that soft shoulder, to kiss it, taste it, whipped through him. She tugged the shirt back up but his urge did not dissipate.

"Pippin?"

She pressed her lips together.

"What were you running from? Won't you tell me?"

She settled down on her pallet, pulling up her blanket and huffing a breath. "Trust me. You doona want to know."

But ah. He did.

He did.

It was a shame that—as stubborn and determined as he was to wrest information from her—she was equally obdurate about sharing. At least about this. At least now.

Maybe one day she would tell him.

Not today, apparently. She muttered, "Good night," closed her eyes and pretended to sleep.

That was, indeed, one way to end a conversation.

Ah well. He settled down on his blanket and gazed up at the open expanse of the sky. It was a dusky plum and spotted with myriad points of light. There were so many stars up there, winkling down at him. It was a sight he'd beheld many times before. For some reason, tonight it filled him with an unfamiliar sense of peace.

It was easy to imagine that somewhere, in the vast and infinite reaches of time and space, all possibilities existed.

Even the possibility of redemption.

Or forgiveness.

Dare he hope?

He shot a glance at Pippin, merely a slight lump in the murky night. Something in the region of his heart tightened, but it was not a painful sensation. It was a pleasant burn. A rightness. He had finally spoken to another soul about the day that haunted him. Shedding light on the darkness had somehow sent shadows skittering away. Some of them at least. It had felt...good talking about it. Talking to her. It felt good being with her. For the first time in nearly a year he felt...himself again.

He knew, somewhere deep in his soul, helping her, keeping her safe, escorting her—at least as far as Inverness—wouldn't wipe away everything he had done and failed to do. It would not scrub his slate clean. But it was a way to begin. And it suddenly felt very, very necessary.

With that thought, he drifted off.

It took some time for Fia to fall asleep. She kept running their conversation through her head, trying to imagine the battle, trying to imagine Graeme in it. Trying to make peace with his death.

Her heart ached for Daniel. It was clear in his voice, the anguished lines of his face, he had still not recovered from that day so long ago. His tale had been woven with agony and angst, yet she suspected there was so much more he had not shared. Could not share.

Finally, she drifted off. It was nearly dawn when a cry awakened her. At first she thought it was the cry of a wolf or an animal in pain. It was a low, keening cry filled with sorrow and torment. Her pulse lurched. She held herself still and tried to hear past the blood rushing in her ears.

When it came again, she knew at once it was indeed the cry of an agonized creature, but not a wolf. If came from the other side of the clearing. She sat up and focused on Daniel's sleeping form. He moaned, grunted, thrashed. And then he cried out once more.

The poor dear was in the claws of a horrific nightmare.

She couldn't, in good conscience, allow him to suffer it.

She threw off her blanket and crept over to him, studying his features in the dim light of the dawning day. His beautiful face was contorted. His lips tight. His nostrils pinched. Sweat beaded his brow. He froze, then lurched. His muscles quivered.

"No," he whispered as his head whipped from side to side. "No."

She set her hand on his shoulder. "Daniel." A plea. "Daniel, wake up."

His eyes snapped open and he skewered her with a savage glare. With a roar, he lunged up and slammed into her, pinning her to the hard, cold ground with a force that made the breath gush from her in a painful whoosh. His weight was stultifying, crushing, punishing. Still wrapped in the trails of his dream, he snarled at her. "No."

Though fear gripped her bowels, though his expression frightened her, she tried to remain calm. She cupped his cheek and stroked him soothingly. "Daniel. It's all right. It's over."

He stared at her. His brow lowered as though he was struggling to comprehend her words, her meaning.

She'd had nightmares before and she knew how haunting they could be. She skated her thumb over his cheek, wiping away the tears clinging to his skin. "You're safe now." It was the only thing she could think to say.

The words seemed to reach him. His body lost some of its rigidity. His hold on her softened a tad. The wildness in his eyes receded. "Safe?"

"Aye. You're here. With me. With Pippin. In Scotland."

He blinked. His gaze raked her face and settled on her lips as though in doing so he could better read her meaning. "Pippin?"

"Aye." She ran her fingers through his hair. It was meant to be a soothing gesture, but she couldn't deny the pleasure of the caress. His hair was silky; his scalp was warm. Her fingers tightened.

And then *he* tightened. His muscles locked. His gaze gained intensity once more, but it was a very different brand of it. He took her chin in his large hand and held her still. His head descended.

With something of a shock, she realized he intended to kiss her.

With a greater shock, she realized just how much she wanted him to.

His lips, when they took hers, were not soft or gentle or seductive. The kiss was a maelstrom. A desperate claiming. A ravenous, rapacious reveling. She had the sense it was not her lips he was claiming, rather a chunk of his soul he had somehow lost.

He savaged her, possessed her, filling her with his scent, his need, his tongue.

She'd been kissed before, but never like this, with such a welling and demanding hunger. And she'd certainly never been kissed by a man so attractive. A man who made her heart race and her body tingle. The embrace swept her away. Stole her sanity.

She couldn't help but respond. When she opened her mouth to him, he shuddered and sank into her, framing her face and holding her, but allowing his fingers to curl through her hair, to tease her neck, to cling.

His other hand swept lower and claimed her breast. When his thumb scored her nipple, a wave of desire swept through her and she arched into him. He groaned and rubbed against her. A hardness at the crux of his thighs gouged her. She knew what it meant and she gloried in it.

He wanted her. This man. This beautiful, wounded, perfect man.

And heaven help her. She wanted him.

In her previous world, such a thing, such an embrace, such an exchange would be unthinkable, scandalous. But that world was dead and gone. She wasn't saving herself for a marriage that would never happen. There was no need to stop him and indeed, she didn't care to. She wanted, needed, ached for what he seemed inclined to give her.

It only seemed polite to encourage him.

As he kissed her—now working his warm, wet lips over her cheek to nest in the sensitive skin of her neck—she allowed herself to explore. Let her hands rove.

And heavens, he was magnificent. Beneath the cotton of his shirt, his skin was hot; his muscles bunched and shivered to her touch. His shoulders were broad and strong, his back firm, his waist tapered and slim. His buttocks...

Was it wrong to mold them in her palms?

He reared up at that and pinned her with a ferocious look. He made a feral noise, something like a growl, and shifted downward. She hadn't realized it, but he'd somehow managed to unbutton her shirt. His hand was scalding as it scudded over her chest and captured a breast.

It was an exquisite claiming. She quivered as his hold enclosed her. But then, oh, mercy, then he lowered his head and took her nipple between his lips...and sucked.

She'd never experienced such a thing. Shards of absolute delight danced on every nerve, whipping through her in a scorching tide, making her body ache and swell. When he nipped, scraping her with his teeth, she nearly came undone. She howled and clenched at his head, holding him there, begging, pleading, panting for more.

And he gave her more.

In fact, he went quite mad, frantically sucking her, stroking, nibbling, moving from one breast to the other. As he worked her, as he plied insanity upon her, his hand drifted lower. With a bolt of tingling awareness, she realized he was working the buttons of her breeks.

She knew she should probably stop him, but she didn't dare. She didn't care. He worked his way ever downward. And then he touched her...there.

She seized.

He touched her there, between her legs, in a spot that suddenly held every secret of the universe. Exaltation exploded in her as he nudged that throbbing button. Pleasure spiraled out with each stroke, each tease.

He grunted and lowered his head again, barraging her nipples and her pearl in tandem. A knot formed in her belly. It blossomed out, filling her with an unbearable tension.

"Please," she cried. "Please!"

His frenzy increased. Like a man possessed, he worked her, drawing her higher and higher into the maelstrom of his passion. And hers.

When she thought she could bear it no more, when she thought she would surely expire from the agonizing bliss, she snapped. Something released within her. A liquid heat gushed through her, from her, and ecstasy, unlike anything she had ever known, descended.

And with that explosion, that implosion, she spun away into a world of colors and lights and absolute rapture.

It was, in a word, perfection.

CHAPTER SEVEN

As Daniel gazed down at Pippin's exquisite face, shock rocked through him. Shock and exhilaration. Because what was this, this feeling he'd so long been denied? This excitement? This desire? This proof of life?

He couldn't believe what he was feeling. He'd been convinced the French lance had unmanned him. But now, here, in the arms of this lovely, responsive, vulnerable girl, he felt it. For her and her alone.

A swelling need. A burning desire.

An erection.

He should stop.

He knew he should stop, but Daniel couldn't bring himself to do so.

It was excuse enough that she had awoken him from a truly horrendous dream and then he, still caught in the tendrils of terror, had taken her down. Once he realized she was not the enemy, that it had indeed been naught but a dream, that the horror was truly over...he'd been suffused with an incomprehensible wash of relief, of joy. And with that swell of overwhelming emotion, something he had not known for months.

Lust.

Because there she was, beneath him, caressing him, cooing in his ear. He'd been beset with the irresistible desire to kiss her, to claim her, to take what he needed.

And he had.

He had not expected her response.

A receptive passion, a warmth. A welcome.

It had been glorious making her come, watching her come.

He should stop.

Really he should.

He would have—he was a disciplined man, after all. He would have rolled away then, suffered this raging, aching arousal. That in itself was a joy, this validation that he was not half a man. Knowing he still *could*.

Aye, he would have let her go then, left her pure, left her innocent and untouched, had she not reached for him. But she did. Her hand was tiny, but he felt it. Felt it with every fiber of his being when she closed her hold on his cock and tugged. And then, God help him, she smiled.

"We shouldna," he grumbled, though he didn't mean it. His blood was high, the passion nearly blinded him. Need raged.

She ignored him—thank God—and stroked him again. Little white stars danced before his eyes.

"Please."

A lovely word.

And ah. He knew. He knew then he would take her. But only because she said please. And he would be gentle. She was a tiny thing.

He yanked off her breeks then yanked his down and settled himself between her legs, fisting his cock and pointing it to heaven. As he brushed her damp folds, her heat scalded him.

He lost his mind. All thoughts of gentility fled.

He lunged.

Absolute agony scored him as he drove deep. Not because she wasn't ready — oh, she was. Her sheath was wet and warm and welcoming. Perfect. And not because as he seated himself, her nails dug into the muscles of his shoulders.

But because she closed on him. *Closed on him.* And ah, God. It was agony.

And ecstasy.

He leaned up and braced on his arms and, pushing back on the clumps of grass for leverage, he eased out. Staring into her eyes, he took her, again and again.

The sensations rocking his body were blissful and divine — surely it had never felt this magnificent before — but it was more than that. It was her gaze, locked to his as it was, her huffs, her sighs, her shivers that drove him on.

"Aye," she moaned. "Daniel. Daniel."

His name on her lips ratcheted his need higher and higher and he had to increase his pace. He wanted to take it slow, to make it last, but he could not. His hunger was far too sharp for patience. And Pippin incited him.

She did so in small ways. The dance of her fingers on his ass, the heinous clutches of her body on his, the sounds that came from her throat. Sounds of a woman in bliss.

His body tautened. He knew it, felt it, recognized it, the familiar and long-absent crisis. Excitement skittered through his veins, rose, lifting him with it, and her as well.

He moved more quickly, with blinding speed, whipping in and out of her body with a scorching ferocity.

His pulse pounded in every pore. His balls shrank into tight nuts. Heat walked up and down his spine. A boiling need grew.

He thought to pull out when he came, to protect her from any consequences, but as he neared his crisis, she came again. Her body seized. She wailed and gripped him tight, holding him in.

The impending doom descended, taking him, waking him, washing him away in a great flood of delirium.

He released to her, in her. Released it all.

Not only his seed, but his fear, his regret, his unrelenting guilt.

Everything he was. Everything he would ever be. He released it all in that moment to a tiny, fragile woman with the unexpected strength to bear it.

As he collapsed at her side, panting, shivering, boneless, he realized that for the first time in nine months, for the first time since that battle that had broken and enslaved him, he knew peace. A deep, abiding peace that filled up all his empty places and made him feel at home in his own skin.

It was what he had been searching for.

He'd found it again.

At last.

At last.

Fia lifted up on her elbow. She couldn't hold back her smile as she looked down at Daniel. Her lover. And my, how wonderful it had been. How wonderful *he* had been. She drew her fingers through his hair and his eyes opened. His lips tweaked in a sleepy smile. He tugged her down, upon him, holding her close.

Thank God she hadn't needed to save herself for marriage, because if she had, she might have missed this. Every touch, every kiss, every whisper was burned on her memory. She would carry it with her all her days.

She wanted to do it again. And soon.

She was utterly flummoxed when, after he had recovered, he levered up and set his hands on her shoulders and gazed into her eyes and said, in a regretful tone, "I am so sorry."

Fia blinked. Her heart threatened to take a tumble but she scolded it not to dare. She wouldn't be sad about this. She would not cry. She forced a smile. "Why are you sorry, Daniel?"

"I shouldna ha' done that."

Oh dear. Tumbling threatened. "I found it rather fine."

He reared back. "Fine? It was a damn sight better than fine." Ah yes. That made her feel better. "But I shouldna ha' done that." She disliked that he turned away. She wanted to see his face.

"Why?"

"Why?" He whirled around. His eyes were wild, red rimmed. "I nearly ravaged you."

She sniffed. "I've been nearly ravaged before and this was nothing like that."

His nostrils flared. His lips worked. His gaze flicked down her body and settled between her legs. She glanced down and saw the evidence of her deflowering, a slight stain on her thigh.

"I said *nearly* ravaged." It seemed prudent to clarify.

She wasn't prepared for his response, a thunderclap of fury. "Who nearly ravaged you?" This, said as though he was the only one with right to do so. But then, in her estimation, this was so.

She shrugged. "Just someone."

Daniel's fists closed. "Is he still alive?"

"I imagine. I beaned him with a chamber pot. He probably survived." Probably.

His eyes narrowed. "Empty or full?"

"Half and half."

He grunted as though this were half satisfying enough. But then his expression darkened once more. "I still canna escape the suspicion that I have taken advantage of the situation. Of you." He waved at the spot where he had absolutely ravaged her—not *nearly* at all. "You were an innocent. A hapless traveler—"

"Hardly hapless."

"I vowed to protect you."

She snorted. "You did no such thing."

"I swear to you. I did."

Her ire rose. "You called me a *nuisance*."

He cringed. "I'm sorry for that, Pippin. You are no' a nuisance."

She put out a lip at his mollifying apology. She didn't want to be mollified. She wanted him to kiss her again, but he seemed to be retreating from her. And all because he imagined he'd betrayed his stupid honor. "You never vowed to protect me," she grumbled.

"I did. I vowed it to myself." He set a hand on his heart, which was altogether too endearing. She had to look away.

"I doona need protection, Daniel."

"You're a woman. Traveling alone. In this world, you do." He raked his hair, savaging it with rough fingers. "And I... Oh God. I..."

She couldn't help it.

She smacked him.

Not hard, but with enough force to capture his attention. "I. Liked. It."

It seemed as though he would soften then, smile maybe. Take her in his arms and kiss her again. Do *that* again... But his chin firmed. It was a lovely chin with delicious scruff and a disarming dent, but she hated to see it firm.

"I liked it too, Pippin, but we canna do that again. As glorious as it was—"

"Oh! Was it glorious?"

"You know it was."

"It was for me. But I dinna know if it was for you." She fluttered her lashes because in his reflection of how glorious it had been, he seemed to have forgotten he was in the process of rejecting her. "A man like you? A man of the world? You must have had many women." As she said the words, her stomach lurched.

Well, hell. He probably had. She didn't like that in the slightest. She tried not to scowl, but feared she failed.

His lips turned up, though not in a mocking smile. Oddly, it was somewhat sad. Certainly sincere. "Nay, my Pippin. I havena had many women. Not many at all. In fact, I..."

She waited patiently for him to continue. Or not so patiently. "You...what?"

He cleared his throat. Glanced away. "I was...injured in the battle."

She set her hand on his shoulder, if only to have some kind of contact, show him her sympathy in some small way. He covered it with his own, which she liked. She liked it very much.

"I was gored by a French lance." He looked even farther away, if that were possible. "In the groin. I haven't been able to... I haven't had... I haven't felt..." He blew out a harsh huff. "There hasn't been a woman for over a year."

She had no idea why delight skittered through her. Or she did. But then she frowned. "And before that?"

He whipped around and gaped at her. "I...what?"

"And before that?" she repeated primly. "Lots of women before that?" Not that she was jealous. Not that she absolutely needed to know.

For some reason he laughed. For some reason he took her in his arms and kissed her. A quick buss filled with inappropriate humor. "No, not lots before either." He caught her expression and winced. "Doona misunderstand. I'm no monk. But Pippin, I am hardly a catch."

He was wrong. He was a brilliant catch.

Would that he could be *her* catch.

"My father was a soldier. My mother a maid. We were people of little means." She didn't understand the shadow of anger that passed over his face, so she ignored it. "My father died when I was young and my mother took ill. I worked from the age of fifteen to put food on the table, to get medicine to make her comfortable. There was little time for romance. And then, when she died, I joined the Greys." He chuckled. "No time then for certain. So there have been few women indeed." He leaned closer and set his forehead to hers. "And none as glorious as you."

Excellent. "So when can we do that again?"

She should have kept her mouth closed. He lurched back. Grimaced. "We canna."

"But it was *glorious*." Did he honestly need reminding? Already?

"It was wrong. And Pippin..." His expression shuttered. "I dinna protect you."

"I have no idea what you mean."

"I should have pulled out. There could be...consequences."

Oh heavens. She hadn't even thought of that. For a girl with no money, no family, no home, a child would indeed be a disaster. But... "Are there ways to prevent such things?"

He gave a pained grimace. "That is hardly the point."

"Are there?"

"Aye. There are, but Pippin, my honor willna allow me to use you."

"U-use me?"

"Aye." He shrugged. "I have nothing to offer. Nothing. I can barely meet my own needs. I canna keep a woman and I wouldna see you suffer in poverty the way my mother suffered."

She laughed. She had to. The sound seemed to stun him. "I'm penniless too, Daniel. I doubt you could lower my circumstances a whit."

"A child could."

A dour reminder.

She shook it off.

"I'm a grown woman." She ignored his dubious perusal. "You're a grown man. And we desire each other…" She trailed off. "We do desire each other, do we no'?"

"I desire you." A begrudging admission. "But it would be wrong for me to lead you on."

"How are you leading me on if we both understand what this is? What is so wrong with using each other? For comfort? Companionship?" Glorious escapades? "If we want to enjoy relations, we simply should. Although…" She peered at him from beneath her lashes. "We should take those precautions."

Holy hell, she was a tempting little minx. And her arguments made sense which, in and of itself, was evidence that he was sinking into insanity. But then, his ardor, now reawakened, had risen with a vengeance. Even now, even sated, he wanted her. Wanted to hold her and kiss her and nuzzle that delicious spot on her neck that made her mewl and thrash.

He thrust the thought from his mind. Thrust the urges from his soul. They clung.

Her scent, wafting to him on the dawning breeze, made it difficult for him to recall his reasoning, his logic.

Ah, but there was no logic when it came to her, he found. No logic whatsoever.

Funny, wasn't it? Just a few days ago he'd been locked in his cage, thinking himself impotent and worthless. Thinking himself all alone.

Today the world was a different place.

He was not sure why.

"Well?"

Apparently he'd delayed too long in his response to her question. Indeed, had there been a question? He couldn't recall. The lure of her presence had wiped his mind clean. A slate erased of everything but her.

"Well, what?"

"When shall we do this again?"

Damn, but she was insistent. And damn, but he wanted to succumb.

His rusty honor prodded him. She'd been a virgin. She needed time to recover. Aside from which, so did he. "Let's play it by ear, shall we?"

She reared back. Apparently she did not care for honor.

He frowned at her, but he tried to make it a gentle frown. "It's nearly daylight. We should get moving if we want to make it to Moulin. Shall we eat breakfast on the road?"

She crossed her arms, which was unfortunate, because it drew his attention to her breasts — which were still bare — and set up within him an unholy howl. "I should like to finish this conversation. If you doona want me then just say so and—"

"Doona want you?" Did she not understand? He wanted her more than anything. More than the honor that defined him.

And that horrified him.

"Well? Do you?" The hint of vulnerability, of doubt, of sadness in her eyes raked him.

He leaned closer—vowing this would absolutely be the last kiss of the morning—and set his lips to hers. "I do want you, Pippin. I do. But we are not doing that again. Not here."

Her face crumpled into a confused rumple. "Why?"

"I shouldna ha' taken you on the ground. Not the first time."

"But I loved it."

"How could you have?"

"It was…earthy."

Of course it was earthy. He'd taken her on the fucking ground. "You deserved better."

"It was perfect."

It had been. He couldn't disagree. "But you deserve better."

She tipped her head to the side. "So…not now?"

He had to laugh. He had no idea where it came from because this was hardly a laughing matter. "Not now."

She nodded, but it was with a pout. And then she stood and dressed—he tried not to wail as her silky skin disappeared—and began packing her things.

He was gratified that she finally understood. That she would give him the time and the space he needed to work out these new feelings, this maelstrom of emotion.

For surely, she had set his world on its ear.

CHAPTER EIGHT

WHILE FIA WASN'T PLEASED THAT DANIEL WAS STILL reticent, she was gratified that, as they rode on the pleasant road to Moulin—munching on apples—his gaze kept drifting to her. Licking her, in fact.

She was suffused by memories of their interaction, remembering, reveling in the recollection of his touch and imagining what more there was to come.

And more, there would be. This, she vowed.

Despite the fact he felt it was dishonorable and wrong for him to seduce her again, he'd said nothing whatsoever about her seducing him. So she did.

All day.

Practically all day.

She'd never seduced a man before, but it was surprising how quickly she picked it up. It was as simple as a glance, a certain kind of smile, an innocent comment about the desire for a vigorous ride.

Occasionally, she brushed against him, letting her leg touch his. When the opportunity arose, she would touch his arm or stroke his hand.

His glances in her direction became more frequent, his expressions hungrier, his frustration more patent. He shifted frequently in the saddle.

She reveled in his discomfort.

Though she was uncomfortable too. Her body ached in ways it never had before and the constant rub of the saddle on suddenly tender flesh was annoying. Each move sent twangs of awareness through her. It was as though he had awakened a part of her body that would not go back to sleep. She was on fire with a desire that was far too new to her.

She glanced at Daniel. He stared ahead with a pained look on his face. He grunted and readjusted his seat. His gaze caught hers. "Are you all right?" she asked.

"I'm fine." A lie.

"Well, I am not."

His head jerked up. "What's wrong?"

She sighed. "I doona know. This has never happened before but I am...warm." She flicked a look at him.

He blinked. "Warm?"

She gestured to the spot where her groin rubbed against the leather. "Here."

He paled. He might have choked on his breath. "Oh God, Pippin. I'm so sorry. I didn't realize..."

"Realize what?"

"What an ogre I am. How could I no' have thought how tender you might be?"

Oh, she was tender all right.

"Shall we stop? We can find a brook for you to soak in. Something soothing?"

She laughed. "It's not a painful kind of warmth." Well, it was. But not painful in the way he meant. "It's more like...a hunger."

Every muscle on his face froze. His chest rose. His thighs tightened, causing Hunnam to dance restlessly. "H-hunger?"

She leaned forward. "Is that...normal?"

"Normal?" A squeak.

"To want you again? So soon?" She fluttered her lashes. "I doona want you to think me a wanton."

"Wanton?"

It was adorable the way he repeated every word she said as though he couldn't come up with thoughts of his own.

She tipped her head to the side and shot him a taunting grin. "It was rather glorious after all." She dabbed at her lips with her tongue.

His gaze locked on it. His Adam's apple worked. A flush crawled up his face. His fists tightened on the reins.

"So is it normal?"

"Normal?" he croaked.

"To want you again? Honestly, Daniel. You must pay attention. Is it normal for a woman to want a man again so soon?"

He made a sound that might have been human. She decided to prod him harder.

"I especially enjoyed it when you kissed me here." She touched her nipple and when a now familiar delight washed through her, she moaned.

His eyes crossed.

"Though I loved when you touched me here too." She allowed her hand to trace its way down and down, to that spot between her legs. He tracked the movement.

"Pippin..." His voice was harsh, pained.

"Should you like me to kiss you *there*?" She peered at him curiously. He appeared to be strangling on something. "Do women *do* such things?"

"Pippin, please stop talking."

"But I'm curious."

"You're killing me with your curiosity."

"Do you think we can try that? When we get to Moulin?"

"Pippin, please." Something of a wail.

She affected a pout, but she wasn't put out in the slightest. Her teasing was having just the effect she intended.

Indeed, he flicked the reins and the horses launched into a trot.

Daniel was mortified. Not only had he taken her virginity like a cad, he'd done it in an orchard. On the ground. Not only had he been so swept away—by her scent, her cries, and the excitement sizzling through his body—that he had ignored his code of honor...he wanted to do it again.

Now.

All day.

Aside from that, if he didn't know better, if he didn't know beyond a shadow of a doubt what an innocent she'd been, he would swear she was attempting to seduce him. But she couldn't be. She couldn't be. He must be interpreting those sidelong glances through the haze of his seething desire. Her comments could not be the ribald jests, the lurid lures, they seemed to be.

No doubt insanity had claimed him.

He wanted to tip her off her horse into the heather and take her there.

Hard, hot and unrestrained. He wanted to cover her like a stallion and thrust his cock into her warm and willing body. He wanted to make her scream. He wanted to make her howl. He wanted to make her yank on his hair as she had so many times this morning.

Had it only been this morning?

It seemed much longer ago. Far too long ago. He wanted to take her again.

But he couldn't. What shreds of honor he still retained wouldn't let him.

Oh, he would fuck her again. He would have her. As often as she would allow. He knew this to the depths of his soul, despite the fact his mind kept insisting he should not.

But not in the heather. Not in an orchard. Not on the hard, cold ground.

She deserved better, his wee Pippin. She deserved romance. A meal. A soft bed.

She deserved a better man than he.

But he decided not to focus on that. She was here with him now, and she wanted him now. Tomorrow, or whenever they parted, she could have that better man. For now, she was his.

The thought exhilarated him...until he remembered that tomorrow was, always and ever, only a day away.

They reached Moulin much sooner than he expected. In time for lunch, in fact. And even though it was far too soon to stop for the day, they did. There was quite a stretch between here and Newtonmore with no inns, and he didn't want to miss the opportunity to savor her in comfort.

He procured a room for them to share and ordered a bath to be prepared while they ate. It was a lavish extravagance, but she deserved it. After they saw to their horses, they joined a small collection of travelers in the common rooms and enjoyed a savory stew.

The company was fine; there was much conversation and jocularity. Daniel smiled and nodded and pretended to be engaged, but all he was aware of was the warm weight of the *boy* by his side. And the fact that a small foot was toying with his.

It made his blood burn.

She was a minx, no doubt. But he would pay her back.

And she would love it.

The instant her bowl was empty, they headed straight up to the small room on the second floor.

The instant the door closed, he whipped her into his arms.

And ah, her mouth. So soft, so supple, so sweet. She tasted of ambrosia. He wanted to sink in and stay there forever. But kissing her—as delightful as it was—was not enough. Not now. Not after the morning he'd spent, in hell, wanting her.

He walked her back toward the bed, his hands moving in a flurry to touch her, caress her, undress her.

Her hands were busy too and soon their clothes fell to the floor. He pulled her against him, sealing them together, reveling in the soft curves of her sweet body. "Ach, darling," he murmured as he buried his face in her hair, supped on her neck, stroked her delicious backside.

She wiggled against him and when he leaned back to scold her, she shot him a disarming grin. "There's a bath," she said, gesturing to the large tub, wreathed in steam, by the fire.

"Aye." His mood fell, just a tad, because he realized he wouldn't be having her quite yet. It wouldn't be fair to fall upon her again like a savage beast, at least not until she'd had her soak. "I ordered it for you."

"Oh!" Her eyes lit up and she pulled from his arms—he was not wont to let her go—and skipped over to swish her fingers in the water. "How divine."

He couldn't halt the swell of pride that he'd provided something so pleasing to her. "Go on. Get in." He watched with an indulgent smile as she slipped into the water; it turned to something else altogether when she moaned. It was a feral moan, an animalistic moan, one that stirred something bestial within him.

As she slid down into the swirling water, he stalked over to her and picked up the cloth the innkeeper had left on the table. "Shall I wash you?"

Her eyes flew open at his sultry tone. He saw an illicit interest flicker there. "W-wash me?"

He knelt beside her and made a lather with the soap. "Shall I?"

"No one's ever washed me before."

"Excellent. I rather like being the first." They shared a smile at his jest but then he realized it wasn't really a jest. It was God's honest truth.

She sobered as well and their gazes clung as some arcane message passed between them. "Yes." Her answer. To so many things. Spoken and unspoken.

He dunked the cloth in the water and proceeded to wash her. Her arms, her shoulders, her beautiful neck. Her breasts. Surely they were not that much in need of cleaning? But he found himself fascinated by the ever tightening crests, so pink and tender and sweet. When she wailed her frustration at his teasing touch, he shifted to her feet and her legs and her belly and then, when he could bear the suspense no longer, he found the place between her thighs and rubbed her there.

Poor thing. She was nearly mindless by then, panting and moaning and twitching restlessly. Her eyes were glazed over and her lips worked, issuing sounds that might have been pleas.

He tried to be diligent. Truly, he did, but he found that he was bereft of patience. He wanted, needed to touch her more deeply. He abandoned the cloth and stroked her barehanded, skin to skin.

Glory, she was wet and warm. Her crease was creamy, her clitoris hard. He circled it and she arched into him with a yowl. She clutched the sides of the tub and braced herself, her muscles stiff, her expression intent. A red tide rose on her chest and flooded her cheeks. Her eyes closed. Her nostrils flared. "Yes," she panted as he drew her closer and closer to heaven. "Yes, yes, yes."

It was delicious to watch, even more entrancing when she broke. Shuddering and keening and writhing in her pleasure. He slipped inside her, filled her with his fingers and played her, toyed with her, strung it out, urging her on and on and on.

It was hard to withdraw when she collapsed in the water, boneless and sated.

But then, everything was hard. He was not boneless in the slightest.

Every nerve in his body hummed and screamed and howled for more. For her. For release.

He stepped into the tub, which thankfully was a large one—scooped her into his arms and settled back down, holding her chest to chest. The warm water engulfed him and he shivered. Her weight on him was lovely. The feel of her breasts pressing against him was magnificent. He held her and stroked her and gloried in it. In her.

It did not take much time for her to recover.

It did not take much time for the minx in her to awaken.

Her hand drifted over his chest and down. She found his cock and encircled it with those tantalizing fingers.

"Mmm." She stroked him leisurely. And damn, he didn't feel leisurely in the slightest. "That was wonderful."

He kissed the tiny hairs curling at her temple. They were damp with her sweat. He licked her and her essence flooded his consciousness. "It was."

She tugged on him and he flinched, though not from any kind of pain. Perhaps some kind of it. "You never did answer my question," she said.

He knew from the tone of her voice there was trouble afoot. "Which one?" She had asked several. They'd all disturbed him.

She shifted up on his lap so she could look him in the eye, but she didn't release her prize. Her grip firmed. His cock lurched. He couldn't resist a tiny surge of his hips. Surely not to encourage more? "Do women ever kiss men *here*?" She traced the tip of his cock.

Shivers danced on every nerve.

His pulse surged.

Oh. Holy. God.

He cleared his throat. "Indeed, they do."

It was alarming how quickly she pushed away and leaped from the bath. "Oh, I want to try." She scrambled for a towel and briskly dried off. Then she handed it to him with a wicked grin. "Come along," she commanded. "I want to try it now."

He could hardly refuse her.

That would have been rude.

He barely bothered with the towel. A quick buff here and there. As soon as he was dry enough to not soak their bed, he sat. His cock, alert and impatient, rose between his legs.

She studied it—from too far away—turning her head this way and that. Her tongue peeped out as she contemplated where to begin and, dear God, he prayed she would. Just begin.

When she knelt between his legs he nearly collapsed— the sight was so beguiling—but he forced himself to hold still. To give her time. Space.

His patience was worth it.

First, she traced his scar with her fingers. It was ragged and thick and dead, but when she bent her head to kiss it, he could swear the nerves sprang back to life.

When she turned her attention to his cock and took him in her grasp and leaned forward and lapped at the head, stars danced before his eyes, a universe of stars. It was beyond perfection. But then she closed her lips on him and suckled. Sucking and sipping at him. And then, she moaned.

She released him, much to his chagrin, but it was to smile up at him and say, "You are delicious."

Ah God. She might just be the perfect woman. "Pippin—"

She cut him off, cut all thoughts off, dipping her head and drawing him in again. How she knew to swirl her tongue like that, to ease down on him, to pump with her fist as she took him in, he didn't know. The pleasure nearly blinded him.

She was too good. He was too needy. It was moving too fast. His head whirled, his body burned. His pulse pounded in his temples, in his cock. A bubbling, boiling need rose within him. He fisted his hands in the covers and gritted his teeth and tried to hold off a rising disaster.

"Pippin..."

He didn't mean to stop her, but he did, and he was glad for it. She glanced up at him again and he realized... "I want you." *I need you.*

Without pause, he reached down and lifted her up, then turned her onto the soft mattress beneath him. Her body was still wet and warm and ready and he had no patience left.

It was time, as she had suggested so often today, to do *that* again.

She loved the look in his eye, the wild hunger, the tender passion.

She loved the feel of him, his bare body, hard and rough, as he covered her. The hairs on his chest abraded her nipples, his hands roved, testing her warmth. His knees fit between hers and with one harsh move, separated them.

It was glorious having him over her, so demanding, so rampant. But she wanted more. She wanted him in.

"Are you ready?" he asked through clenched teeth and she had to laugh.

"I've been ready for hours."

She had no idea why this caused his eyes to narrow, his nostrils to flare, but she hardly cared, because then he lunged. He filled her. Completed her.

As wonderful as it had been this morning, this was better. There was no small pinch of pain. It was pleasure, all pleasure, delirious rafts of it. She was barely aware of his movements over her and in her, because each thrust sent her higher and higher into some ethereal realm where nothing existed but skittering bliss and shards of glory.

She luxuriated in the slide of his hard, velvet spear as he filled her again and again. With each surge, he nudged something deep within her, something that made her soul sing and weep at the same time. A tight ball formed at her core and expanded, creating an unbearable tension. He seemed to know. He seemed to understand. With a growl, he increased his pace, his movements becoming wilder, harsher, more desperate, as though he fought the same beast, climbed the same crest.

He swelled inside her, stretching her even more, sending a riot of euphoria through her. The delight wafted out in wave after wave after wave. Her body closed down, seized, and he groaned. He jerked, several times, and made a noise, something feral and savage and utterly replete. And heat flooded her. Heat and heaven and a breathtaking sense of serenity.

He collapsed upon her and then rolled to the side, taking her with him, holding her close. His chest heaved. His heart thundered. His fingers toyed with her hair.

Tiny moans emanated from his throat. Or the moans could have been hers. They were so close at this moment it was difficult to tell them apart. She hardly cared.

Nestling closer, she kissed him. His neck. His chest. Wherever she was.

They lay like that for an eternity, just holding each other as the day waned. They might have slept. As the room darkened and the sounds of revelry rose from the tavern below, Fia's belly growled. She leaned up and gazed down at Daniel's face. He looked at her through slumberous eyes. His lips quirked. He reached up to tuck a wayward curl behind her ear. "How are you doing?" he asked.

"I'm hungry."

He chuckled. "You're always hungry."

"I am." It was true.

"Shall we dress and go down below?"

She wrinkled her nose. She didn't want to face the world. Not yet. He seemed to understand.

"Or have our supper here?"

"Here, please."

"My choice as well. I shall go down and have them send up a tray." He hefted off the bed and she tracked his progress, enjoying the sight of his perfectly formed buttocks. He picked up his trousers and pulled them on, and then fumbled in the jumble of their clothing for his shirt. As he lifted it up, something fell to the wood floor with a thunk and rolled under the bed.

Fia was closest, so she leaned down and picked it up.

Her heart stalled as she stared at it.

It was a chess piece, a knight, exquisitely carved in a hand she could not mistake for another. She knew it. She knew the lines. She had its mate.

"Where did you get this?" she asked through the ball clogging her throat.

He glanced over, in the process of buttoning his shirt. A muscle tightened in his cheek. "A friend made it."

Her lungs locked. Her pulse thrummed. A sense of inevitability whipped through her like a cold wind. "A...friend?"

"Aye." He glanced away. A surety he didn't want to discuss it, but she had to press him. This was far too important.

"And...what happened to this friend?"

He raked his hair and then sat beside her on the bed. "He died."

"In Waterloo?" She knew. She *knew*.

"Aye." He took the piece and stroked it, then folded her into her arms and held her, with his chin on the top of her head as though he couldn't bear to look at her. "He's the one I told you about. The one I didn't save." A whisper.

Ah. God.

Her soul wept. For so many reasons. For Daniel, for Graeme, for herself. But she only said, "You canna save everyone."

He grunted, a wordless response. And then, after a while, he said, "I'm supposed to deliver it."

She tried to pull back. To look at him. He wouldn't allow it. "To whom?" she said to his chest.

"He had a sister. In Sutherland County." Ah yes. Their home had been there. Until they'd lost it. "I've been...putting it off."

"Why?" she asked, but she knew.

His Adam's apple worked; she felt it against her cheek. "I canna bear to face her." His tone was far too anguished.

She should tell him now, tell him who she was, that his friend had been her beloved brother...but she couldn't. She knew, beyond a shadow of a doubt, if she did, this thing—this brilliant and glorious thing between them—would end. It would end the instant she opened her mouth and she wasn't ready for that. Didn't think she ever would be ready for that. She didn't think she could survive it.

Ah, lord. She should tell him, but she'd never known such fear. Such howling panic. She didn't care for this evidence of her cowardice, but she couldn't deny it either.

Later. She could tell him later. She would.

Just not now. Not yet.

Fia wrenched from his hold and pinned him with a savage glare. "It wasna your fault that he died."

"Even if it wasna, I have to explain it to her. I doona think I can."

She cupped his cheek. "She will understand."

"Will she?"

"Of course she will." She kissed him then, softly, sweetly. "Of course she will." She pushed him down on the bed and he allowed it. "She will," she said. "She will."

She soothed him then, loved him then, with her body, heart and soul.

It was a long time indeed before they had any supper.

CHAPTER NINE

THE NEXT FEW DAYS, AS THEY RODE TOWARD Inverness, were delightful. The evenings were even more delightful. They made camp by the side of the road and he and Pippin spent each night locked in each other's embrace, glorying in the panoply of nature.

The nature of desire to be precise, but Daniel did make an effort to notice the natural beauty of their surroundings…as much as he could. He was rather obsessed with her.

And obsession it was.

Somehow, in that handful of days, she had come to mean so much to him. Not just the woman who had grabbed him by the scruff of the neck and hauled him from the pit of despair. Not just the woman who had, in her miraculous and gentle way, healed his desire. Not just a witty and pleasant companion he would want to have at his side for the rest of his days. But more.

She had become necessary.

As necessary as water or air.

He should be terrified by that, but he was not. He reveled in it, the connection, the closeness, even the need.

He'd never allowed himself to need anyone before. Not even before Waterloo had broken him. When his father died and his mother became ill, he'd become the provider, the savior, the protector. It was his role. It was his destiny.

Somehow, with Pippin, he'd become all those things, and more.

When she looked at him, she saw a hero. It was there, shining in her eyes.

He couldn't help but respond to that.

And in that, she made him a better man.

He didn't allow himself to think of the future. It was too painful. For as much as he enjoyed her company, as deeply as he sank into his need for her, this wonderful affair was only that. It couldn't be anything more.

No matter how much he wished he could keep her, he couldn't. His means were limited, his circumstances occasionally desperate. If not for the charity of other men — men like Worth and Sherstone — he would probably have starved. He was lucky to have a job. Lucky to have a place to sleep. And frankly, the small room he inhabited above the stables of the Incomparables Club in London was no place for someone of her sensibilities. Beyond which, there was no doubt the members of the club would object to him bringing a woman home to live with him.

He resolved himself to the fact that his time with his Pippin was limited. And, as any man would, he made certain to take advantage of the gift that had been given to him.

Regret was for tomorrow.

Today was for something far more pleasurable.

It was almost an annoyance to arrive in Newtonmore and be surrounded by a bustle of people again. Well, hardly a bustle, but certainly more than they had found on the heaths. Aside from which, it had been a long day's ride and they were both creaky. Daniel was thinking about another bath. He was thinking very seriously about it. He also wanted her again. Needed her beneath him. He had it in his mind to drag her up the stairs to their room as soon as he could arrange one, but he didn't have the chance.

He had dismounted from Hunnam and handed the reins to a waiting ostler, when he glanced up at Pippin's face, preparing to help her down. Something in her expression snagged his attention. She was looking toward the inn, her features locked in a mask of disbelief. He followed her gaze and saw a young man just coming out of the door. He seemed to be a carefree sort with a smile on his lips and a laugh in his throat. He strode with a cocksure gait and had a bag slung casually over his shoulder.

Pippin's eyes narrowed.

"Do you know him?" Daniel asked softly.

"Aye." Her tone made a shiver skitter down his spine. "He's the one who stole my things."

The fellow glanced up just then, saw her, and stilled. His face went an odd shade of white. His gaze flicked over the yard and then without warning, he sprinted into the darkening woods.

To his horror, Pippin slipped of Blaze's back—without his assistance—landed on her feet and hared off after the lad.

Daniel stood there in shock for a second and then, almost instinctually, launched into a run in her wake. It was growing dark and the trees were close. He lost sight of her almost immediately. His panic rose as he crashed through the brush. His lungs worked like a bellows, squeezing painfully as he ran.

She was so small. So helpless. Where had they gone? Where was she? What the hell had she been thinking?

A cry to his left turned his blood to ice. It was her cry. He skidded to a halt and, changing directions, barreled through the bushes toward the sound.

What he saw as he burst into the clearing infuriated him, brought down a scorching red tide he hadn't known since Waterloo.

Pippin and the thief tussled over the strap of the bag, each tugging it back and forth, each unwilling to let it go. But then the brigand hauled back and slammed his fist into Pippin's belly, sending her flying.

Daniel roared.

The trees shook. The ground rumbled. His cry reverberated on the air. It certainly took the thief aback. He stilled, frozen in place, gaping at Daniel's oncoming charge.

The boy should not have hesitated. He should have turned tail and run. Because Daniel was furious. His nostrils flared as he flew toward the bastard; his hands closed into fists. He landed a hard blow on a cocky chin. It was a damn good thing Daniel hadn't had his saber in his hand, or he would, no doubt, have run the sod through.

The boy reeled back and collapsed. He didn't move.

It was something of an anticlimax, that. Daniel had been prepared to pummel him to mush, but he didn't move. Daniel nudged him with a toe, hoping the bastard might stir.

Nothing.

A shame. One punch had not been nearly enough, but the notion of beating an unconscious man offended Daniel's sense of honor.

He was aware, through the bloody haze of his vision, that Pippin had edged close and was studying the insensate pile of flesh and bones.

"Are you all right?" he asked.

She nodded. "I'm fine. Did you kill him?"

"Unfortunately not."

"Pity." She bent down and collected the bag from his shoulder and riffled through it. Apparently she found what she was looking for; she turned to Daniel with a bright smile. "Are you ready for dinner?"

"What?"

"I said, are you ready for dinner?"

Seriously? "He hit you. How can you think of food at a time like this?"

"I'm hungry."

Naturally.

Daniel glared at the ruffian once more, just for good measure, and then tucked his arm around Pippin—because surely she required the solicitous gesture—and led her back through the trees toward the inn. As they made their way, he attempted to calm himself, but it took some effort. When he was capable of civil speech he asked, because he had to know, "Why did you do that?"

She glanced at him. Blinked. "Do what?"

"Chase him, for pity sake." Honestly, sometimes he feared this woman might drive him to drink.

"He stole my bag."

"It's only a bag."

"Hunnam is only a horse, but you dinna want him stolen."

"Hunnam is *not* only a horse. And that's beside the point. The man could have hurt you. Really hurt you." Couldn't she see that? Couldn't she understand? Didn't she know how fragile and precious she was?

"But he dinna." She turned to him, her eyes adoring. "You dinna let him." It was shocking how those words, that expression, hit him so hard in the gut. Because somehow, in her eyes, he saw the man he so desperately wanted to be.

He saw a hero.

As they neared the teeming city of Inverness, Daniel's anxiety rose and he knew damn well why. When they arrived in the city, his time with her would be over. It would end. Pippin would continue north, to meet her "people" in Wick, and he would…well, he didn't know what he would do. But it wouldn't be with her.

The thing he most wanted, craved, couldn't be. The thought devastated him. It probably accounted for the desperate passion with which he took her each night. His desolation rose the closer they got. In Kingussie, Inverdruie and Tomatin. Each town, each inn, each step tolled a death knell for this delightful interlude.

Too soon they reached the outskirts of town. The sights and smells of it made something bitter rise in his throat, but he knew it was nothing more than dread.

He chose an inn he knew well, one he was confident would be comfortable and safe. Safety was a key factor in a city this large, filled to the brim as it was with danger. And since he didn't know the location of his uncle's solicitors, it didn't make sense to search for some place near their offices. Aside from all that, he preferred to stop somewhere familiar. They arrived in the early evening, but thankfully there was a room still available and Daniel quickly made arrangements for their dinner and that bath.

They spent a lovely, leisurely evening together, in each other's arms, though they both knew it was probably their last night together. Which most likely accounted for the tears.

He awoke before her and dressed quietly before slipping out of the room and down to the kitchens, where he asked for a tray. She was still sleeping when he returned with it—

poor thing, he had exhausted her — so he set it on the table and sat next to her on the bed. She snuffled a snore and rolled over onto her back.

He stared at her, at her delicately carved features, her soft curls, the exquisite curves of her bare body. His heart clenched, swelled. Though he didn't want to wake her — although a part of him did — he set his palm to her cheek and thumbed her sweet lips. They moved beneath his touch.

Ah, God. She was beautiful.

She was funny and valiant and brazen and naive.

She was a perfect soul.

And he loved her. Loved her.

He was not a praying man, but in that moment he did. He closed his eyes, ignoring the dampness that squeezed out, and begged God for some miracle. Something to allow him to keep her, even though he couldn't imagine what such a miracle might look like. He couldn't envision any possible future where they could be together. Where he could afford a wife.

Doubtless, she would say she didn't care if they had a decent home or not, but he did. He'd seen what poverty had done to his mother and he couldn't bear subjecting Pippin to those horrors.

But still, he prayed. It was all he had.

And then he made another plea to the Almighty, one that was more likely to be answered. *Please, God. Please let her find fulfillment in her life. Let her find that better man. Let her be safe and happy and loved.* Even if Daniel could not be that man, he wanted that for her.

He bent and kissed her tenderly on the brow, drawing in the musky scent of her sleep, the fragrance of her hair, the essence of her soul, and then he stood in a rush and quit the room. He had to, or he might never leave.

It only took a few queries for him to find the solicitor's offices on Young Street near Ness Bridge. It was a gloomy edifice on a gloomy street. Daniel tethered Hunnam and made his way up the steps in a rush. He wanted this over, so he could return to her. So they could spend as much time together as they could. With any luck he could convince her to stay another night with him before she embarked on her northward journey.

He was certain he could.

He pushed into the offices of Mordecai and Fisk and was assailed with the musty scent of old books. The room was dingy and cluttered. Light barely filtered in through the high windows. A slender, elderly, gnomelike man with muttonchops and thick spectacles sat at a desk, behind piles of papers, frowning and muttering to himself. He didn't notice he had a visitor until Daniel cleared his throat. His head shot up and he peered at Daniel like a little furry owl.

"Oh, pardon. Pardon. I beg your pardon." He dropped his quill and leaped to his feet, scrubbing the ink from his fingers on his wool trousers. "May I help you?"

"Yes, please. I'm here to see Ezra Mordecai." Daniel pulled the letter from his pocket and handed it over.

The man scanned it and his fishy lips parted. "Fisk!" he warbled. "Fisk, you must come at once."

A grumble issued from the connecting room and another man waddled into the chamber. With the exception of his roundness, he was nearly a match to the other, sporting even muttonier muttonchops and thicker glasses.

Daniel bit his cheek to keep from smiling.

"What is it, Mordecai?" he asked in that grumbly tone which was, apparently, his natural speaking voice.

Mordecai waved the letter. "It's him. He's come."

"What? Who?" Fisk adjusted his spectacles on the bridge of his nose and scanned the letter. His eyes narrowed and he pinned Daniel with a sharp gaze. Then he snorted. "Well, he took his damn time about it, did he no'?"

Daniel blinked. "I beg your pardon—"

"Oh, do come in," Mordecai interjected, taking Daniel's arm and leading him into another chamber that was something of a sitting room. Unlike the offices, it was quite plush and outfitted with comfortable chairs and had a large bow window, letting in the light. He waved at one of the Hepplewhites. "Please sit, Lord Sinclair."

Heat prickled Daniel's neck. A sudden mortification washed through him. Well, hell. Had this letter come to him by mistake? Had they summoned the wrong Sinclair? Had he come all this way for nothing? "I beg your pardon. I am *Daniel* Sinclair."

"Aye. Aye." Mordecai squinted at him through thick spectacles.

"I'm hardly a lord."

Mordecai looked at Fisk and Fisk looked right back. "Oh dear. He doesna know."

"He doesna know."

"Indeed. I daresay he does no'."

"Know what?"

"I thought we told him."

"I was certain we did."

"Told me what?"

"For heaven's sake, I thought we were clear."

"We were perfectly clear."

"Sirs!" A bellow.

This caught their attention. Their heads, in tandem, turned. "Aye?"

"Would you mind telling me what you're talking about?"

"Lord Sinclair—"

"I am *not* a lord."

"I regret to inform you, your uncle has died."

Oh for pity sake. He knew that. "Yes. I am aware of that." And he'd left Daniel some pittance. "That doesna make me a lord. His son, Fergus, would be the new baron."

Mordecai fiddled with the letter. He and Fisk shared a look and Fisk whispered, "He doesna know."

"I told you he dinna know."

"I thought we told him."

"I'm certain we did."

"*Sirs!*"

They startled and stared at him, their lips working. They might have mouthed, *He doesna know*, or something of the like.

"Will you please tell me what has happened?"

"Certainly. Your uncle has died."

Daniel sighed.

"A massive apoplexy by the looks of it."

"A shame." It was not, but it was a polite lie.

"Naturally, Fergus inherited. The title. The house. The money."

"Naturally."

Fisk narrowed his eyes. "Naturally, he, ah, celebrated."

Disgust churned in Daniel's gut. *He* had not celebrated when *his* father died. But with his recollections of Fergus, he wasn't surprised that his cousin had. He'd been a mean and spiteful boy.

Mordecai nodded. "Stewed himself to the gills."

"There was…an unfortunate incident."

"Involving a horse."

Fisk leaned closer and whispered, "A trampling."

"How…unpleasant."

"Indeed." Fisk nodded. "At any rate, you have inherited."

Daniel frowned at him. "Inherited what?"

"All of it."

All of what?

"The house in Dunbeath, the title."

"The horse."

But... "There was another heir. Callum."

"Humph," Fisk grumbled.

Mordecai leaned forward and set his hand on Daniel's and whispered, "France," as though that explained it all. But then, it did.

It was difficult to process. His uncle and both his cousins were gone. And he was the sole heir to a property he barely remembered. His mind reeled. He'd never anticipated such a thing. Never expected to be anything more than that which he was and always had been. A penniless mongrel.

Uncle William would be turning in his grave.

No doubt the house was rundown and ramshackle. Daniel remembered it being so as a child. And while his uncle had at one time been a man of means, he'd also had the unfortunate habit of living beyond them. He'd been an inveterate gambler, swinging wildly between affluence and penury. It was hard to say on which point on the pendulum he had met his end, but Daniel did not hold on to hope that there would be much left.

But he couldn't still the trill of excitement at the thought...he owned a house. He had *some* money. Something. Surely enough to keep a wife.

Surely enough to keep *her*.

The solicitors droned on, going over the various points of Uncle William's will and elements of the law that took over where it left off. Then they peppered Daniel with a litany of things he must do now, straight away, such as report to the magistrate in Borgue, who could officiate his title and provide the specifics of this benefice.

But he wasn't paying much attention. He was swamped with thoughts of Pippin. With the realization they wouldn't have to part today. This thing between them—whatever it was—was not over. He could escort her to Wick. It was not so far from Dunbeath. Perhaps in that time he could convince her to stay with him instead. Perhaps he could convince her to stay with him altogether.

It was a dizzying thought.

He was so beset with it, he had no recollection of returning to the inn. Indeed, he fairly flew back to her. He leaped from the saddle and tossed the reins to the ostler and was heading inside to find her, to tell her, to hold her when, from behind him, someone called, "I say. Corporal Sinclair? Is that you?"

His steps stalled. His gut clenched at the familiar tones of a dreaded voice. Slowly, he turned. And yes. Indeed. It was he. Lieutenant Grant. Daniel grimaced and then forced a smile as his nemesis approached. They'd served together in the Greys, though Grant had been an officer, and a cocky one at that. He and Daniel had rarely seen eye to eye. Aside from which, Grant was a lord and didn't hesitate to let everyone know it.

He was tall and broad with sand-colored hair, brown eyes and a patrician nose. He walked with a swagger and his lips usually curled with something that could easily be interpreted as a smirk. Beyond which, his manner intimated his superiority to all men, most especially to a corporal beneath his command.

Daniel was not beneath his command now. Still he tendered a respectful bow. "Grant," he said, taking the other man's hand. "Well met."

"Indeed. It is good to see a familiar face," he said, his expression—shockingly—sincere. "What are you doing in Inverness? I'd heard you were staying in England."

"Ah, yes. I'm here meeting with a solicitor."

Grant wrinkled his nose. "Enjoyable."

"Quite."

Daniel started as Grant wrapped an arm around his shoulder and guided him into the inn. They'd never been friends. This show of amity was a shock. "Have a drink with me. We should catch up."

"Ah..." He wanted nothing less. In fact, what he wanted, more than anything, was to find Pippin and bed her again. To tell her his news and offer a proposal that they travel together to the Highlands. But Grant tugged him to a table and lifted a finger to the serving girl and for some reason, Daniel allowed it. Not that he wanted to catch up with Grant. Not that he cared what the man had been up to in all these months, but there was something in his tone, in his expression that echoed in his own soul — a hunger for the companionship of a man who had shared an experience one could not make peace with on his own. Though they were not friends, and probably never would be, an experience like Waterloo bound men together with unbreakable bonds.

So he sat. And accepted a flagon of ale. And prepared to spend some time with a man he had never liked.

"So, Sinclair," Grant gusted. "Do tell. What have you been up to?"

Daniel lifted a shoulder. "Not much. Recuperating."

"Ah yes. Your leg. I see you're walking again."

"A mercy, that."

"Indeed. And where were you staying?"

Good gad, he actually seemed interested. "Worth took me in."

"Ah, Worth. Good man. Good man."

"Indeed."

"And how is he doing?" Was it Daniel's imagination or was there a hint of desperation in the question? In the conversation?

"Rather well."

Grant sighed, something wistful. "Time does heal all wounds, I suppose."

"One would hope."

Grant fell silent and toyed with his cup. He glanced around the common room and then, at length, leaned in and said softly, "May I ask you something, Sinclair?" He seemed so somber, so sincere, Daniel nodded without thinking. "Do you...?" He ran a finger around his collar as if it were too tight. "Do you have...dreams about it?" He didn't need to clarify. Daniel knew at once what he meant.

Something cold traced his spine. He took a quaff of his ale, surely not to swallow down any heinous memories. "Every night." Or nearly so. He hadn't had them since... Well, since Pippin.

Grant blew out a breath and sat back, something akin to relief on his face. "Me too." His Adam's apple worked. "I canna seem to forget."

"Perhaps we are not meant to forget." He didn't want to forget. Not Hamilton, nor Lennox nor any of the others.

His companion's eyes bulged. "Not meant to forget?" Horror tangled in his tone.

"Our memory honors those who fell. Perhaps they live, even a little, in us."

"Oh yes. Yes, of course." Grant let go a laugh that was a trifle manic. "I mistook your meaning." When Daniel arched a brow, he waved a hand and mumbled something about the torments of hell.

Daniel didn't respond. It had been hell, that battle, and in the nightmares he relived it again and again. It had occurred to him that such nightly visitations were a punishment for his acts on the battlefield, payment for all the men he'd killed. But the nightmares were easing. Maybe God had forgiven him. He'd certainly answered Daniel's prayer, providing a miracle right one cue.

It was almost enough to restore his faith.

The two men sipped on their ale in silence, both reflecting on their private thoughts. Their secret regrets. Then Grant cleared his throat. "So, Sinclair, what will you do once your business here in Inverness is finished? I ask because in a few months, I'm hosting a reunion of sorts at Grantham. You might like to attend."

"A reunion?"

"Some of the men from our regiment. Nothing fancy. Simply a...reunion."

A reunion. In a few months. "When?"

Grant cleared his throat again. "June."

Ah. Not a reunion. An anniversary.

"Fitzgerald will be there and Dingle and Crumm."

All good men. He'd liked them very much. "I would enjoy that, if I'm still around."

"Where do you anticipate you'll be?"

Good lord. He had no idea. Not the foggiest notion. "I'm not sure. Tomorrow I'm heading to Dunbeath to inspect an inheritance—"

"An inheritance?" Grant clapped Daniel on the back, causing him to spill his drink. "Good for you. What did you inherit?"

"A house." And a title, presumably, but he didn't care to mention that yet, not until he knew more. Mordecai and Fisk were decidedly blurry on the specifics. Aside from which, Daniel was still convinced that when he arrived in Borgue, the magistrate would laugh and wave it all off as some horrible mistake.

"A house. How nice. Cause for celebration." He raised a finger and ordered more drinks though they had not finished those they had.

Daniel lifted his cup. "I have no idea what manner of house it is. I haven't been in Dunbeath since I was in short pants." It had not been a pleasant visit.

"Dunbeath is lovely. You'll enjoy it there."

"If the house is habitable."

"Indeed. And if it is, and you stay, I should hope you and I might see each other once in a while." He set his hand on Daniel's arm; his expression was solemn. "I could use a friend like you nearby."

Well, they weren't friends, at least they hadn't been. How odd that it seemed as though they might be now. Regardless, Daniel knew exactly what he meant. There were many who understood their wounds, had lived them, but they were scattered all over the globe. There was nothing as comforting as a friend with whom one could commiserate — face-to-face.

"I would like that."

"Excellent." Grant's face broke into a smile, and it was not a smug one in the slightest. It seemed...humble, grateful even. "When do you leave?"

"Most likely on the morrow." No doubt he and Pippin would want to be on their way at once. They still had quite a ways to travel.

"Excellent! I am leaving on the morrow as well. Heading home to Grantham, don't you know. We shall travel together."

Oh.

Hell.

Daniel swallowed. He could hardly refuse this man, this man who might be his friend. His neighbor. But he didn't want to travel with him. For one thing, how long could he keep Pippin's secret? For another, how would he explain it to Grant when, at each posting house, he shared a room with his *companion*?

It could be, indeed, awkward.

But there was no way he could wriggle out of the invitation.

CHAPTER TEN

DANIEL WAS GONE MOST OF THE DAY. FIA SWUNG between fretting that he might not return at all, agonizing over each second with him lost, and glorying in the memories of the past few nights. It ate at her soul that it was nearly time for them to part. If only he would take her with him. She would go with him anywhere.

She could only pray that his uncle had left him something, some small inheritance. Was it selfish for her to hope he had? That he'd left Daniel enough to change his mind about keeping her with him? Although part of her feared that the money might be only part of it. Only his excuse. There was no doubt he'd enjoyed their tangling, but he was a man and men saw such things differently. He might not *want* more. Might not want what she did.

When he finally pushed through the door to their room, she greeted him with a frown. He smiled and wrapped her in his arms and kissed it off her lips. "What's the matter, puss?" he cooed.

"You were gone a long time."

He paused in the process of unfastening his collar. "I'm sorry. The meeting took quite a bit of time and then...I ran into a friend."

"A friend?"

"Aye. We...had a lengthy chat."

"I hope it was pleasant."

He blinked at her starchy tone. "It...was."

"Good." Because honestly. This was their last day together. And he'd spent it with someone else. Her mood took a tumble. "How did your meeting with the solicitors go?" It was the only thing she could think to say.

"It was...surprising."

"Did your uncle leave you a pittance?"

"In fact, he did not."

No. Of course not. She sighed and turned away.

"In point of fact, I inherited everything."

She stilled. Then whirled around. Her jaw dropped. "What?"

Daniel grinned and opened his arms, inviting her in. "I doona know what it all means yet, Pippin. I doona know the details of the estate, but I do know I have inherited a house in Dunbeath. And a horse."

"A house in Dunbeath?" It sounded lovely. Lovelier still was the way his arms closed around her, the glimmer in his eye.

He tapped her on the nose. "Dunbeath is near Wick."

Her heart lurched. Her throat worked. "Near Wick?"

"What do you think about traveling there...together?"

"Together?" She was aware she was parroting his every word, but she couldn't help it. Joy, glorious joy swept through her. "Oh, Daniel!" She reached up and kissed him, a quick, elated buss.

"Do you want to?"

"Want to?" There she went again. "Yes. Yes. Oh yes!"

He picked her up and spun her around. Elation made her giddy. This was not their last day together. Not at all.

It wasn't until they had made love — slowly and leisurely as now there was no rush to speak of — that he dropped the other shoe. "You remember the friend I mentioned?" he murmured against her forehead.

She snuggled closer, draped her thigh over his. "Aye."

He pulled back to look at her. "He's traveling north too. Would you mind verra much if he joined us?"

Her stomach clenched. She tried not to make a face. Because she did. She did mind. She didn't want to share Daniel with anyone. But the man was his friend and judging from his hopeful expression, he wanted her to say yes. She wanted nothing more than to please him so she said, "That would be...lovely."

"Thank you." He kissed her again, his expression solemn, and then it broke into a grin. "It will be difficult to keep your secret from him. He's a clever man." This, he said with a teasing tone.

"I shall attempt to be verra boyish."

Daniel chuckled and then winced as she drew her leg over his erection. And yes, he had one. Again. Her smile blossomed.

No doubt they would be tired indeed come morning.

She didn't care. Because she'd been given a great gift. Her time with him was not done. And that was a magnificent thing.

It was early the next morning when they rose and prepared to undertake the next leg of their journey to the north. Daniel was exhausted — he had not slept much — but he was filled with an invigorating anticipation to see his new home, and a delight that he would be with Pippin, which made up for it.

He and Pippin found Grant in the common rooms, eating breakfast, and after Daniel ordered their mounts to be readied, they joined him. He introduced Pippin as his traveling companion and nothing more. Grant didn't seem to have an inkling that she was anything other than what she presented. A young boy traveling north.

She was quiet during the meal other than to make token attempts at conversation; he could only assume she was tired as well.

It took all of his attention to remember not to kiss her or stroke her hand or put his arm around her.

This journey might well be a trial indeed.

He contemplated just telling Grant the truth about her; he doubted he had the wherewithal to keep up the subterfuge for very long.

The sun had not yet risen and the trails of morning fog wreathed through the street as the small party headed for the stables where their mounts awaited. As they neared, Grant's steps stalled. His eyes narrowed. He approached Pippin's horse and held out a hand. The mare nuzzled him. His gaze darkened as it met Daniel's.

"Is this your horse?" he asked in a sharp voice.

"Nae. The grey is mine. This is Pippin's."

Grant's attention whipped to her with such ferocity, she stepped back. "And where did you come by such a beautiful animal?" He attempted a casual stance, but his intensity hummed.

Pippin pressed her lips together and then said, "A friend gave her to me."

"Oh, really?" Grant's tone made the hair rise on Daniel's nape. He stepped forward, to put himself between them, even as Grant added, "Do you know what they do to horse thieves, boy?"

It was frightening the way she paled. The way something that could have been guilt flickered over her features. It made Daniel's gut coil. It would be bad enough to discover that one were abetting a horse thief. Even worse to think that his Pippin might have committed a hangable offense.

"I dinna steal the horse," she snapped. "I only borrowed it."

Before he could stay the words, he said, "The way you borrowed the apples?"

She shot him a look that made him flinch. It was threaded with a wounded outrage. She crossed her arms and glared from one man to the other. "A friend let me borrow the horse."

"*This* horse?" Grant's brow furrowed.

"Aye. This horse."

Grant eased closer. There was a predatory glint in his eye that made Daniel's belly lurch. "Which friend?" And when Pippin's expression became mutinous, he added, "Best tell me, boy. Because I know this horse like I know the back of my hand, and I know for a fact she doesna belong to you. Tell me who loaned her to you or I will call the constable and have you arrested for thievery."

The bloody hell he would. Daniel bristled. His fists closed. He opened his mouth to object, but then Pippin spoke. Only two words, but they poleaxed him.

"Chelsea Grant."

Holy God. Grant's sister.

She knew Grant's sister?

How on earth did she know Grant's sister?

Grant reared back, apparently as stunned as Daniel.

Pippin riffled in her bag and pulled out a paper, which she waved. "I have a letter."

Eyes narrowed, Grant snatched the parchment from her hand and scanned it. As he read, he stilled. His lips parted; his jaw dropped. He glanced at Pippin and scoured her with an intense scrutiny, then shot a look at Daniel and paled. His lips worked. He gestured in Pippin's general direction, sputtering, "But...but...but..."

She propped her hands on her hips and blew out a breath. "It was Chelsea's idea."

Grant raked his fingers through his hair, mussing it irreparably. "Good God. That does sound like her." And then, "Does *he* know?" For some reason, Grant nodded in Daniel's direction.

It was then he realized that the letter had revealed her spurious gender.

"He knows," he said in a growl.

She shot a look at him and his bile surged...because the look she sent him was one of chagrin. Possibly pity. She lapped at her lips. "He doesna know...everything."

Daniel's pulse surged. He nearly swallowed his tongue. "What do you mean, I doona know everything?" Of any man in Scotland, hell, in the British Isles, the world, he should be the one to know everything about her. He should be the only one.

Grant crooked a brow at Pippin and when she nodded, he handed the letter over. Daniel read it quickly and...

God.

Oh God.

The earth dropped out from beneath him. His knees locked and he nearly crumbled.

Charles, darling.

Please take charge of my dear friend, Fia Lennox, who has found herself in dire straits since the death of her brother in Waterloo.

The first thing that occurred to him was that her name was Fia. It was a lovely name. But then, there on the heels of it...*Lennox.*

She was Fia Lennox.

Dear God.

I know you understand her circumstance and that, if the tables had been turned, if you had died instead of Lieutenant Lennox, you would want the same protection for me.

Daniel's fingers closed on the letter. He stared at Pippin—*Fia*—through a shimmering haze. "Your brother was Lieutenant Lennox?" It wasn't meant to be a question, but lord help him, he needed some confirmation from her. Something.

She nodded. "I'm sorry I dinna tell you, Daniel."

Something in his gut lurched. "You *knew?*"

"When I saw the chessman. Aye. I knew it was Graeme's."

Oh lord. He felt faint. Something howled in his head. It might have been the devil laughing.

Damn the house in Dunbeath. Damn any pittance of inheritance. None of that would make any difference at all. None of that could change anything at all. No fortune, not even a fucking castle could make up for the fact that he was not worthy of her and never would be.

Because he was a horrible man.

He had seduced his best friend's sister—his *innocent* sister—a girl he was honor-bound to protect.

Hell. He had not merely seduced her. He had debauched her. On the ground. In an orchard. In a bathtub. Time and time again.

And she? She had given herself to the man who was responsible for her brother's death. When she realized the truth of it—as surely she would—she would walk away and never look back.

And he couldn't blame her.

Funny how one little revelation could change everything.

The swiftness of it, the absolute and utter finality of it, made Fia's head spin.

The look on Daniel's face left no doubt in her mind she'd been right to keep her true identity from him. And wrong at the same time. The little lie had bought her a little more time with him, but it was clear he was done with her.

His jaw had firmed, his features tightened, his nostrils pinched. The revulsion in his expression as he studied her with cold eyes was horrifying.

Even worse, there was no chance to speak with him about it. About anything.

Once Charles realized who she was, and assumed responsibility for her, he didn't waste any time becoming dictatorial. Chelsea had warned her, but Fia hadn't realized just how overbearing he could be.

The first thing he did was insist—*insist*—she not ride Blaze. He rented a carriage and tied the mare to the back and nothing Fia said would change his mind. Not even her insistence that she preferred to ride.

"Nonsense," he said in response.

He said that a lot.

Fia didn't like the carriage. She didn't like the way it jolted on the rutted road, she didn't care for the isolation and boredom—as both the men continued to ride—and she most especially did not care for the smell. But when she opened the window and poked her head out, Charles scolded her.

Scolded her.

She was a grown woman, for pity sake. Chelsea should have put *that* in the letter.

He even had the temerity to suggest buying her proper clothes, but Fia put her foot down at that. For one thing, trousers were much more comfortable when traveling.

Beyond all that, Fia was frustrated. She wanted to speak to Daniel — in private. His reaction, when he'd realized who she was, who her brother was, had ripped her to shreds. Fear raked her. Fear that he was furious with her for keeping that secret, fear that he wouldn't be able to face her now that he knew. Fear that he was in pain. With each step, each breath, he drifted further and further away.

But there was no opportunity for conversation. For one thing, he rode outside, and for another, Charles was ever present, hovering over her like a father hen.

When they stopped at the first inn in Urray, Charles bustled her in as Daniel tended to the horses. Chelsea's brother had Fia ensconced in a private room with supper and a bath before she knew what had happened. And while she did appreciate the bath, it was hardly glorious. She was all alone. She wasn't even allowed to dine with the men. Charles insisted the common rooms in the evenings were not a fit place for a woman of her stature.

The argument that Fia no longer had any stature didn't seem to penetrate his thick skull.

She would have crept to Daniel's room once the shadows of night fell, but she overheard the conversation between Charles and the innkeeper, and she knew her two traveling companions were sharing a chamber.

Damn.

Damn and blast.

Frustration railed.

She tried to force herself to sleep so she could rise early, preferably before Charles, and have a chance to talk to Daniel alone, but she couldn't. She lay awake, staring at the ceiling, feeling terribly alone and bereft, trying desperately not to notice the music and laughter wafting up from below.

At least someone was having fun.

The Urray inn was a busy one. The dining hall was bustling and filled with rough and ready men tucking into a hearty meal. Daniel and Grant were no different, although Daniel found he had little appetite. While he was thankful Charles had insisted Fia stay in her room and away from this boisterous crowd, he missed her.

It occurred to him that he might just as well get used to the misery.

Their glorious affair was over. He tried not to think on the fact it should never have happened in the first place. He tried to ignore the howling evidence of his perfidy.

It occurred to him, rather belatedly, that he should have pressed her for her real name when he realized she wasn't a boy. Hell, he should have pressed her for the name of her dead brother when they spoke of Waterloo. But in truth, he hadn't asked because he hadn't wanted to know her brother's identity. At the time, he'd been wreathed in apprehension that the name would be a familiar one and that would have scraped him raw.

As it turned out, it would have been familiar indeed.

Had he known she was Lennox's sister, he would never have touched her. He wasn't sure if he should curse his ignorance or celebrate it.

"Well," Grant said as he lifted his tankard of ale. The word sliced between them like a saber.

Daniel tried not to flinch at his tone. "Well."

His friend pinned him with a sharp look. "How long have you been traveling with her?"

Ah yes. He knew this was coming. It had probably been simmering all day. "A week. A little more."

"And?"

Holy God. Was Grant looking for a confession? He would not get one. For one thing, it was none of his damn business. Daniel narrowed his eyes and snapped, "And what?"

"I see the way she looks at you."

"And how is that?"

Grant snorted. "She's besotted."

Was she? What a lovely prospect.

Grant's glare, not so much. "I consider myself her guardian now. The letter and all," he said, though this was hardly a shock, given his proprietary manner with her; it made Daniel's hackles rise. If anyone had call to be proprietary with her, it was he.

"She is her own woman."

"I'm aware of that." Grant smiled, but it wasn't a smile. Not really. "I think it only fair to warn you. I intend to be diligent in my protection of her."

Daniel bristled. He hated being warned. Especially about this. About her. Besides, *he* had been diligent in his protection of her—most of the time—and he resented the inference that he had not.

Grant ignored his outrage. Though it was possible he hadn't noticed it. It had been turned inward, after all. "She is Lennox's sister." Daniel hardly needed reminding. It still howled through his soul. All day, he'd struggled to make some peace with it. "That alone marks her as a woman to be treated with honor."

"I have treated her with honor." Something of a lie.

"I'm sure you have, Sinclair. You always were an honorable man." Thank God Grant's intensity eased. "But given the glances flying between you, I felt it needed to be said."

Was it wrong for his impatience to simmer so? Were roles reversed, he'd be grilling Grant with the same rhetoric. "And now that it's said?"

His friend shrugged. "We drop it."

Excellent. Daniel didn't want to hear about it, think about it, stew about it anymore. He refilled their tankards. He nearly spilled the pitcher when Grant said, "So, how did the two of you come to travel together?"

Hell. So much for dropping it. "She was robbed and had no money for food. I fed her." There. That was honorable.

"I see." Grant glanced down and traced the lip of his glass. "Did she tell you how she came to be traveling alone on the road? The letter dinna say."

"She dinna share much of that, other than to say she was running away from a place she dinna want to be. She, ah, mentioned being accosted there."

Grant's muscles bunched. "At the school? At Dunready's?"

"I assume."

"Hell." His expression went feral. "My sister is at that school."

"You'd best ask her about it."

Grant nearly growled. "You'd best believe I shall."

The conversation faltered then, which was a blessing...and a curse. For the rest of the evening and well into the night, Grant was in a foul mood. Neither of them got much sleep at all, but for very different reasons.

CHAPTER ELEVEN

The NEXT MORNING, FIA TRIED TO WAKE UP EARLY, with the hopes of finding Daniel alone in the common rooms, but she failed. For one thing, Daniel wasn't there. For another, Charles already was. He sat at a table by the fire, attacking a plate of ham and eggs as though it were a dread enemy in desperate need of hacking. He looked like a disgruntled beast, with a tight, fierce expression and hair that stuck up in all sorts of wayward directions. Dark circles arced beneath his eyes and he grumbled to himself under his breath.

She considered taking another table, but Charles saw her and waved her over. When she hesitated he glowered.

As she took her seat, he pinned her with a look; she winced at his intensity.

"Fia," he barked with no preamble whatsoever. "Why did you leave Dunready's?"

She blinked. Annoyance rippled in her gut. "Good morning to you too," she said in a syrupy voice. A maid brought her a plate and she lit in. Charles's frown hardly dissuaded her at all.

"Good morning. Why did you leave Dunready's?"

She sighed. "Must we discuss this now?"

"We must."

"I'm eating."

"Sinclair said you were *accosted*."

Fia pointed at her plate with her fork. "Eat-ing."

"I must know. Is Chelsea in danger?"

Of a sudden, her irritation with him evaporated. His fury wasn't directed at her. He was simply worried about his sister. As he should be.

Fia set down her fork. "Chelsea is quite safe, Charles. He would never bother her. Or any of the other girls. 'Tis only the servants who have to worry."

Charles made a strangled sound. "He?" And then, "He who?"

"Blackbottom's nephew. He has an unfortunate penchant for taking what he wants from the helpless within his reach."

His brow darkened. His fists closed. "I canna have my sister at an establishment that employs such a creature."

Fia tried not to laugh, but it burst from her anyway.

This earned her a scowl. "What is so funny, pray tell?"

She lifted a shoulder. "Judging from what the other servant girls told me, such creatures are everywhere. They see the working class as fair game."

"That is utter ballocks."

Fia stiffened her back and folded her hands in her lap. She met his eye. "Is it?"

The flush rising on his cheeks made clear he knew it was not. It was not ballocks in the slightest. "I shall bring Chelsea home at once."

Was it wrong to feel a trill of excitement at that? She'd missed Chelsea these past weeks. It would be lovely to see her again.

Daniel joined them before Fia could respond, and he stole all her attention. As horrible as Charles looked this morning, Daniel looked worse. It was as though neither man had slept a wink.

"Good morning, Daniel," she said. "How did you sleep?"

Lord, she hated that his lips tightened, his gaze flicked away. "Fine. I trust you slept well...*Fia.*"

She flinched. Not because it was the first time she'd heard her name on his lips, but because of the harsh tenor in which he spat it. As though it tasted bad.

No doubt he resented her lie, but it had been a necessary one.

But then...had it?

Surely she should have told him earlier. Could have told him. Before he discovered it the way he did. She should have told him when he discovered she wasn't a boy. But she had not. She wasn't sure why.

She simply couldn't blame him for being angry.

When Charles got up to refill his plate, she leaned over the table and whispered, "I'm sorry, Daniel."

His gaze met hers; his was darkened by a lowered brow. "What?"

"I'm sorry. I should ha' told you who I was when I realized you knew Graeme."

She didn't expect him to growl. Didn't expect his expression to grow harsh, pained. "You've nothing to apologize for," he hissed. "It is I... I'm the one who should ha'..."

"Who should ha' what?"

"Treated you with honor. I'm mortified. Ashamed of myself."

"Ashamed?" She didn't like that in the least. "Are you saying you dinna enjoy..." She made what she hoped was an illustrative gesture. "It?"

He blanched. "Of course I did. That's hardly the point."

"It is exactly the point, Daniel. I mean—"

"Your brother was my *friend*."

"And?"

"And I... And we... We did...what we did."

"Aye. We did." She had to smile. His befuddlement was too adorable.

He scowled at her. "I shouldna ha' done it."

"Well," she said primly. "I am verra glad you did. I enjoyed it verra much."

"But Graeme..."

"I daresay Graeme would have approved."

His nostrils flared. "I assure you, he would not!"

She waggled her fingers at him. "Pish."

"I believe we established *pish* is no argument at all."

"Pish. Graeme would have approved."

"He would *not* have."

"And why not?"

"Isn't it obvious?"

"No."

He went red. A tide of it rushed up to the tips of his ears. "Because," he said in something of a croak. "I'm no' worthy of you."

She gaped at him. Couldn't help it. What utter ballocks. "You are the finest man I know."

"You must not know many men."

Well, that was true, but also beside the point. "Daniel Sinclair, I canna think of another soul I would want to spend my time with, be with. In that way. In any way. I hold you in the highest esteem. And if you and Graeme were friends, he would have felt the same way."

He didn't respond. Simply stared at her with a sad look in his eye. It sliced her like a blade. She swallowed heavily. Her throat hurt. "Do you even want me?" she asked, hating the desolate wind blowing through the words.

"You know I do, but…"

"But nothing." She put out a lip. "You want me and I want you. Is that not enough?"

Nothing. No answer at all.

A sudden fury prickled through her. "Do you know what this is, Daniel? Nothing but your pride." His silly, stupid pride. "And pride goeth before the fall."

He reared up. His nostrils flared. "Pride?"

"Aye. Pride. That, or apathy."

"It is not apathy!"

"Pride then. I hope it keeps you warm at night."

"Fia, you doona understand."

"Och. I understand. I understand perfectly." She stood and tossed her napkin onto the table. A cold ball settled in her belly. Frustration raked her. He was letting his guilt over Graeme's death be an excuse to let her go. To push her away. To end this. And, to an honorable man, as he was, it was excuse enough.

"Fia!"

"Nae. Nae. I willna listen to one more word of this." She spun away and bumped into Charles, who was returning to the table; he blinked in surprise. "I shall be waiting in the carriage when you are ready to leave," she snapped, and then she rushed from the room, nearly blinded by the tears in her eyes.

Silly, wasn't it, to have their first fight over something like this?

Something that could end it all?

Guilt was, indeed, an insidious foe.

They barely spoke again all the way to Borgue. It was the most miserable few days of Daniel's life. Ah, but then it got worse. When they arrived in Borgue, he asked the innkeeper, a portly man named Potts, to give him the magistrate's direction because he intended to meet with him at once and see this dismal business finished once and for all.

The response was a rumbly laugh. "At once?" Potts said with a grin.

"Aye."

The man leaned in and gouged Daniel with an elbow. "Do ye no' know nothing happens *at once* in Borgue?"

"What do you mean?"

Potts chuckled. "The magistrate is Laird Dunn and he's away on a hunting trip in Bower."

Damn. Damn and blast. "How long will he be gone?"

"Well now. Seems to me that depends on the game, now don't it?" He winked. "Could be a week. Could be two."

"Two weeks?" Panic whipped through him. He didn't know why. Oh hell. He did. It had nothing to do with the magistrate and his ill-timed hunting trip. Somewhere deep in his heart, he'd hoped to have this thing settled today. He'd hoped for confirmation that this was all some big mistake and he was *not* the Daniel Sinclair who had inherited a house in Dunbeath. That he still had no means. That he was absolutely not the man for her.

That he was right in letting her go.

That there was some honor in letting her go, rather than naught but a toxic mix of guilt and pride.

That would make it so much easier, letting her go.

Or not.

But now he had none of those things. He simply had…letting her go.

And today.

With no warning.

Oh, he'd known this day was coming, he'd seen it creeping ever closer, but he was still not prepared.

"Will you stay with me while I wait?" he asked Grant, even though he knew it was a stupid, pointless, anguished plea.

Grant grimaced. "I canna. I need to get to Grantham and make arrangements to bring Chelsea home at once." He pulled out his pocket watch and checked the time. "If Fia and I leave now, we can make it to Lybster by dark and then it's a short ride to Wick."

"Of course. Of course." Daniel tried to make his voice casual, but he was sure no one missed the break in it. He swallowed heavily and turned to Fia. Too soon, too quickly, it was time to say good-bye. "I..." Dear God. He couldn't think what to say. *I love you? I want you? I need you?* "I have enjoyed traveling with you." He cringed. Even to his own ears the words sounded hollow and patronizing.

She didn't seem to notice. Her lashes fluttered. Her lips worked. "And I...you."

"I wish you...the verra best, Fia."

"And I you." Their gazes met. Heat sloughed through him. A desperate hope, a hopeless wish rang through his soul. This couldn't be good-bye. It could not be.

But it was.

"Will you come and see me?" she asked in a whisper. Her eyes were wide, round, damp.

"I shall." A tender lie.

Grant, barely able to contain his impatience now that he was so close to home, handed Fia into the coach. It clawed at Daniel's soul, clawed out a chunk of it, watching her step into that carriage.

"You will see him in June," Grant said in a cheerful voice that held only a tinge of impatience. "He's coming to the reunion. Are you not?" They'd talked of it often, but Daniel didn't think he would, even if he found himself living in Dunbeath. He didn't think he could bear it. Seeing her again.

"I shall try."

Though Grant seemed to sense the prevarication, he didn't push. He closed the carriage door, but Daniel's gaze stayed locked on Fia. She sat stock-still, stiff as a board, staring ahead sightlessly. The vision scored his soul. He tore his gaze away and walked Grant to his mount. His friend thrust out a hand. "Well, it was good seeing you again, Sinclair. Good traveling with you. I wish you well with your inheritance."

"Thank you."

"You are welcome at Grantham any time."

"Thank you. And Grant?"

"Aye?"

"Take care of her?"

Grant's smile faded. His grip tightened. "I will."

"She deserves a husband. A good man. A better man than I."

His friend snorted and shot a look at the carriage. "I doona think she wants another man."

The observation sent shards of pain through him. "She'll forget me. In time."

Another snort.

"Just see what you can do to help her find happiness."

"You know I will. It could have been any of us who died that day. Any of us watching from the other side, hoping someone we trusted took care of those we loved."

Well fuck. He didn't need to rub it in. Daniel was already miserable enough. With his heart like a stone in his throat, he watched as Grant snapped his reins and sprang forward, with the carriage carrying Daniel's heart and soul following in his wake.

Fia trembled from holding herself still, from forcing her muscles not to wrench open the door, from holding back her agonized sobs as the carriage lurched. This was it. This was good-bye. This was the last time she would see him. Ever.

She was certain of it.

Damn him and damn his pride. Damn his honor.

Why could she not have fallen in love with a dishonorable man? One who was not bound by such stringent convictions about right and wrong?

Because he wouldn't have been Daniel then, a voice whispered in her heart.

She told it to shut up.

"Wait!"

Her pulse skittered as his voice cried out, halting the coach. Joy, absolute joy, pure elation gushed through her. She poked her head out of the window and shot him a glowing smile. Daniel. Her Daniel.

He ran to her as the carriage slowed, stopped. "Fia..." he said, as he set his hand on hers.

"Aye?" she said on a soft breath. For heavens, he had changed his—

"Here." Expression harsh, brows lowered, he thrust something at her and, without another word, turned and walked away. He did not look back.

Her elation staggered, then fell.

As the coach pitched forward once more, she glanced at the item he'd given her, the exquisitely carved knight her brother had made her. The one Daniel had been holding. The one he'd promised to deliver to her. The one that completed her set.

But she was not completed. She was not completed in the slightest. She, in fact, was bereft.

It was a full two weeks before the magistrate returned from his hunting trip, though, apparently, it had been a successful trip. He was in a brilliant mood when he found Daniel having breakfast in the common room of the Borgue inn. A tall, robust man with ginger hair and a ruddy face, he greeted Daniel with a hearty handshake and a slap on the shoulder. "Well, Sinclair. It took you long enough," he said, by way of greeting. He took his seat and lifted a finger for a tankard of ale.

"I beg your pardon?"

"The Laird of Dunbeath has been dead for months now. Well, both of them. The father and the son." He chuckled as though this were amusing.

"I, ah, had to come from London."

"Well, I must say, I'm relieved to see you."

"Are you?"

"Ach aye. For one thing, I'm damn tired of managing your estate."

"My...what?"

"Beyond that, I wasna sure what kind of man the new baron would be. A sniveling popinjay or some such." He pinned Daniel with a sharp study. "Are you a popinjay?"

"I doona believe so."

"I've heard tell you were in the Greys?"

"Aye."

"Good. Good. No popinjay. Tell me, Sinclair, do you hunt?"

"Do I...what?"

"Hunt? Your uncle dinna. It would be fine indeed to have another local laird to hunt with."

Daniel's impatience sizzled. "I beg your pardon, Lord Dunn. But I have some questions about this inheritance."

Dunn sat back and blinked. "Questions?"

"Aye. Mordecai and Fisk were…not forthcoming on the details."

"Bah. Those old codgers. They never are. But there's not much to tell. Through a series of unfortunate incidents, you are the heir of Dunbeath. The title, the estate, the house…"

"The horse."

"Aye." Dunn chuckled again. "Magnificent filly, that one. Fergus should never have abused her. But she got her own back, I daresay."

"Indeed. But… Are you sure it is I? There is not some other heir?" Some other cousin? Some other Daniel Sinclair? For some reason, he still couldn't accept the fact that this had happened to him.

"Are you William's nephew? From his fourth-born brother?"

"Aye."

"Then it is indeed you." Dunn sobered. "I know this is a lot to take in. Would you care to see the house?"

Excitement, and fear, coiled in his gut. He swallowed heavily and nodded.

No matter what happened now, his life would never be the same.

Somehow, miraculously, he was a laird. With an estate. And a house in Dunbeath.

A house in Dunbeath, the hell.

It was a fucking castle. Or near enough to one. Even now, weeks after taking up residence, taking up the reins of his estate — his fucking *estate*, for God's sake — Daniel still got lost on the way to the privy.

He'd been confused at first, when Dunn had shown him the house. It wasn't anything like the dilapidated wreck he remembered as a child. But Dunn explained that after William had won this manor, and the fortune that came with it, in a card game, he'd had the old house demolished. The estate included vast lands, a herd of sheep, a shipping concern and a village.

A village.

In a heartbeat, Daniel had gone from being a pauper to a man wealthier than he ever could have imagined. Funny how difficult the transition turned out to be. He had so much to learn. Not the least of which were the names of his servants.

There was an army of them.

Maids and footmen and cooks and pastry chefs. He thought it a trifle ostentatious to have so many people at his beck and call, but Dunn had explained—when Daniel had wanted to thin the herd—that these people needed the work, and Daniel could certainly afford them.

Aside from that, the estate was vast. It even had an apple orchard. Too often, he found himself there, drawing in the spicy scent and staring wistfully up into the boughs. But he couldn't allow himself to think of Fia. If he thought of her, he might weaken. He might start believing that his new circumstances made him a better man. Wiped away his sins, his failures, the spot on his soul.

Nothing changed who a man was at his core. Not wealth. Certainly not a castle.

"My lord."

Another thing that was difficult getting used to.

Daniel turned to Grayson, his butler.

He had a butler.

"Aye?"

"A letter for you, my lord." He held out a silver tray — one that would feed a family for a year.

"Thank you, Grayson." Daniel took the parchment and studied it. Good God. It was from Grant. He didn't know why his heart slammed in his chest.

Oh hell. He did.

"Will you be riding today, my lord?"

"Riding?" He picked up his letter opener, one fashioned after a cavalry sword, and sliced open the seal.

"Yes, my lord. Will you be riding today?"

Was the letter about Fia? Was she well? Was she happy?

Had she found that better man?

A cold fist gripped his chest. Sweat prickled on his brow. He couldn't bear it. He couldn't.

Did it really matter that he was a terrible person? That it was his fault her brother had died? That he had seduced her mercilessly? A number of times? In various positions?

And it had been glorious?

Did it?

Of course it did.

He set his teeth and quickly scanned the missive for her name and nearly crumpled it into a ball when he didn't see it, only some falderal about the coming reunion and a query as to whether or not Daniel would attend. *Blast.*

He'd wanted…he'd wanted so badly to hear about her. Something. Anything.

Wick wasn't so very far away —

"My lord?"

"What?" There was no call to snap. Grayson reared back and Daniel cringed. "I'm sorry. What?"

"Shall we prepare your horse?"

"My horse? Yes. Please." Damn it all to hell, he needed a ride. Something wild and taxing. Something that would exhaust him and clear his mind. Something that could make him forget he'd ever held her, kissed her, met her.

Well, not that. He didn't want to forget that.

God, he missed her. It was an ache in his soul.

But at least she was safe. At least she was with Grant.

At least she was free to find a man who could make her happy.

It couldn't be him.

It shouldn't.

CHAPTER TWELVE

*O*H. HOLY. GOD. IT WAS TORTURE.

Fia had had no idea it would be so horrific, or she never would have come to Wick. She would have refused Chelsea's invitation and thrown herself on the mercy of the court. Surely Newgate was better than this.

This was awful. Beyond belief.

She hunched lower beneath the bower and held her breath. Her heart thudded. God help her if he found her...

"Fia? Fia? Where are you?"

She winced as his voice wafted through the garden. Damn. He was here.

"Fia?" Coming closer.

It was Dingle. He was the worst. She hunched lower still.

Still he spotted her. His eyes glimmered. He stepped toward her. "There you are."

Damn.

"What are you doing in the bushes?"

Hiding. It should be obvious. But then, Dingle was not the sharpest arrow in the quiver.

He was also not the most attractive arrow — in the quiver or elsewhere. It was probably ungracious of her to notice, but though he was a noted hero of Waterloo, he had a weak chin. She did so prefer a strong chin. Square. Covered with black bristles. Dented in the center.

Not that anyone specific came to mind. He did not.

Not in the slightest.

Aside from that, Dingle had nostrils. Cavernous nostrils. As his nose was slightly upturned, a small woman, such as Fia, could see all the way up into his brain. Or so it seemed. He also had the unfortunate habit of salivating through his words. Everything he said was *wet*. It was rather disarming.

Suffice to say, of all the men attending Charles's reunion house party, Dingle was one of her least favorites. Probably on account of the inadvertent spray. Although, if she were being honest, none of the men here truly registered as prospects, despite the fact that most all of them seemed inclined to court her.

And Charles, damn him, was determined to find her a husband. He paraded one prospect after another before her in an endless stream. Not one of them held a candle to the tall, valiant cavalryman who had ruined her for all others.

It had been a relief when Chelsea arrived, and not only because Fia had missed her friend. But because Chelsea could assume some of the suitors. Dingle, perhaps...

"I do say, Miss Lennox, Fia, if I may call you that." She forbore reminding him he already had. "I was hoping we could take a stroll together beside the loch."

She smiled. Or grimaced. Whatever. "That would be lovely." She glanced at the sky, searching for the lightning bolt that would surely strike her down.

Dingle took her arm and she attempted valiantly not to flinch.

As they strolled to the loch, he pattered on about this and that and whatnot. Fia nodded and murmured something vague and encouraging on occasion, but she wasn't listening. There didn't seem to be a point.

There didn't seem to be a point in much, these days.

Odd, wasn't it, how desolate she was? Now that her future was secure? Charles had assured her of that, that he would feed her and clothe her and help her find a decent husband. She would never have to worry about anything again.

How odd that life had been much more exciting when she'd been unsure.

But then, Daniel factored greatly in that excitement.

She missed him terribly. Every day. And she had to acknowledge, had she not been thinking of him each and every day, all day—and all night—Dingle or Fitzgerald or Crumm or any of Charles's other friends might have seemed more appealing.

Pity Daniel was the only one she wanted.

Pity he didn't want her. At least, not enough to overcome his damned pride. Or his guilt. Or whatever excuse was keeping him away.

If he wanted her—really wanted her—he would have come by now.

Charles had invited him to this party. He could have come. She could only assume he had not because she was here.

Which was ballocks.

"Fia! Fia!" She glanced up and, with great relief, saw Chelsea making her way across the lawn, one hand on her bonnet, as the breeze had sprung up.

"Oh thank God," she said under her breath.

"I beg your pardon?" Dingle sputtered.

"Look, it's Chelsea. Isn't she lovely?" she gushed.

"Not near as lovely as you, Miss Lennox."

"Nonsense. She is *much* lovelier." She leaned in and clutched his arm. "And I understand she has a generous portion." Wicked of her, tossing her very best friend to the wolves, but honestly, she'd had quite enough of Dingle's spittle.

"Oh Fia, darling. I've been looking for you." Chelsea's eyes were large as she approached. "I do apologize, Mr. Dingle," she said with a curtsey and a smile in the general direction of his nostrils. "But I must steal Fia from you. There's something to which we must attend at once."

Dingle's face fell—which had an unfortunate impact to that crumbling chin—and released her. "I say. That is a shame. We were having such a charming conversation."

Well, *he* had been.

"Maybe another time, Mr. Dingle?"

"Wonderful."

Not if she could help it.

He kissed her hand and she was thankful for the gloves Charles had provided. Still, they came back damp.

She nodded to him and hooked arms with Chelsea and they fairly flew toward the house. "What is it?" she asked, breathless at the pace her friend set.

"What is what?" Chelsea gusted.

"What is it that we need to attend to at once?"

"Oh." Her grin was naughty. "Nothing. I just thought I should save you from him."

Fia's heart swelled, and then a pang of guilt shafted her. It occurred to her perhaps she shouldn't have tossed Chelsea to the wolves after all. "Thank you."

"I canna help noticing the way your nose wrinkles when he approaches."

"It doesna," she said as they stepped onto the portico of the sprawling mansion that was now her home.

"Aye, it does." Chelsea laughed. "I canna blame you, though. None of them are so verra scintillating, are they?"

"They are not."

"Which is why you should consider Charles."

Oh dear. Not again. "Chelsea, darling…"

"He is handsome, is he not?"

"He is."

"And wealthy. And charming. And a good, good man."

"I am certain he is."

"He is. Valiant and heroic as well." She waggled a finger. "Only consider how he dealt with Blackbottom's nephew."

"I'm sure Horace shall enjoy life at sea."

"Charles did that for *you,* darling."

"I rather think he did it for *you,* Chelsea."

"For all of us then. No matter. It was valiant and heroic."

"Aye. He is valiant."

"And heroic."

"That too. But…"

Chelsea sighed as they stepped through the French doors and into the morning room that looked out onto the garden. "It's *him,* isn't it?"

Fia glanced away. She'd told Chelsea everything, well, almost everything. At the very least, she'd shared that she'd met a man on her travels and she very seriously feared she'd lost her heart to him. Chelsea believed Charles was the cure. He was indeed a wonderful, generous, caring man. But he was not. Not the cure. Certainly not Daniel.

No one was.

"Fia, you canna mourn him forever."

"I doona intend to." Just until she ceased to draw breath.

"You need a husband. You need to forget him."

What folly was that?

She would never, could never forget him. She thought of him all day and dreamed of him at night. In fact, even now, as they stepped into the hall, she could see the outline of his familiar form shadowed in the doorway.

Her steps stalled. Her breath caught. Her heart stuttered.

The shadow removed its hat and coat and handed them to the equally shadowy butler, who then shut the door, closing out the blinding light. Fia blinked, willing her vision to clear, but when she opened her eyes, glory, there he was, standing in the foyer, tall and broad and solid and real.

Not a dream at all.

When she let go the breath she'd been holding, her head went dizzy and she sank to the ground as darkness rose up to meet her.

That could not be Fia.

Not that angel in a beautiful frothy dress with her curls arranged in such a stylish fashion, her eyes shining and lips parted.

Daniel stared at her, soaking her in, exulting in the sight of her.

She'd been adorable in trousers and an overlarge shirt, but dressed as a woman, exquisite.

Unable to stay still, he took a step toward her, her name on his lips. But before he could reach her, she went an odd shade of white and crumpled. Thankfully, the woman standing beside her—had there been a woman standing beside her?—caught her and eased her down.

"Fia," the woman said, patting her gently on the cheek. "Fia."

Heart pounding, Daniel rushed to her and knelt at her side. "Fia, darling." He lifted her against his chest, cradling her. God, it was wonderful holding her again, drawing in her scent, feeling her warmth, the beat of her heart against his. But still, fear barraged him, making his skin go clammy. Was she all right? Was she ill? He shot a fierce glower at the woman and opened his mouth to bark some query.

Before he could, Grant's booming voice echoed in the hall. "I say, Sinclair. What have you done to Miss Lennox?"

Daniel flinched and shot a glare over his shoulder at his friend. His *maybe* friend. "And hullo to you too."

Grant waved off his scold with a flutter of his fingers. "What happened?" he asked.

"She fainted," the other woman said. Daniel glanced at her and realized, to his surprise, she was rather lovely as well. But then she turned her gaze on him and scowled and he thought he might want to revise his opinion. "She saw *him*, and fainted."

"Understandable," Grant said. "He is rather horrifying." There was no call for him to chuckle. "By the by, Chelsea Grant, meet Daniel Sinclair. Sinclair, my sister, Chelsea."

Chelsea's eyes narrowed on Daniel's face. "You're *him*?"

"I, ah… Him, who?"

In response, she smacked him. It wasn't a hard smack and only to the shoulder, but he felt it.

"Shall we just leave Miss Lennox on the floor or do you think at some point we might want to move her somewhere more comfortable?" Honestly, sometimes Grant was an ass.

Daniel sucked in a deep breath and lifted her up. She was like thistledown in his arms.

Chelsea led the way to a sitting room filled with comfortable chairs and Daniel settled Fia on the divan. He knelt beside her and took her hand in his and stroked it, gazing at her precious face. She was so still, so pale, it startled him. "Could we get her some water?" he asked.

Charles nodded to Chelsea, who flushed. "Oh, yes. Of course." She whirled in a flurry of skirts and hurried from the room. Once she was gone, Charles arranged himself in a

Hepplewhite, draping his leg over the arm, and fixed Daniel with a sharp look.

"What are you doing here?" he asked.

"You invited me."

"Aye. But you declined."

Daniel scowled at him. "I changed my mind."

"Because you wanted to attend the party?"

"Naturally." Such a lie. For the last month he'd been haunted, tormented, suffused with thoughts of her, memories of their time together, a blinding craving for more time with her. Forever with her.

One morning, as he'd been banging around his enormous and empty castle — utterly alone — it suddenly hit him.

It didn't matter.

Nothing mattered.

Not money or honor or choices or regrets.

Nothing mattered if a man was all alone. If he had no one to share his life with, his hopes, his fears, his dreams. He'd suddenly seen what she'd been trying to say. He'd seen the walls he'd built to keep everyone out, to keep her out.

They worked. They were strong. Indomitable.

And they walled him in as well.

He had to break them down. He couldn't live like this. Not cold and alone and bereft.

He loved her. Needed her.

And he'd been a fool. A proud, lonely fool.

He found himself on his horse that morning, before he knew what had happened, heading up the north road for Wick. With that decision, some weight on his soul had lifted and he knew he would not, could not return to Dunbeath without her.

He only hoped it wasn't too late. Only hope she hadn't forgotten him. Or given up on him. Or found someone else.

"There's no other reason you came?"

Was Grant still in the room? Was he still talking? "Sod off, Grant." Daniel shot him a glare and his friend's lips tweaked in that annoying smug smile.

"I say, this is rather inconvenient. Having you show up like this with no warning."

"You *did* invite me."

Grant ignored this salient fact. "I've been working verra diligently to keep my promise to you, you know."

"What?"

Grant fluttered his fingers in Fia's general direction. "To find a suitor for her."

Something very nasty coiled in Daniel's gut. Was he too late? Was there someone else? A growl emanated from his throat.

"I am her guardian, after all. It's my responsibility to be sure she makes a brilliant match."

"She's mine." A snarl from the depths of his soul. It echoed in the room, feral and desperate.

There was no call for Grant to laugh as he did. "Honestly, Sinclair. I'm not sure you're the right man for her."

"What?" Every muscle bunched. Who the hell else was there?

"She's made quite a splash with our old compatriots." He leaned forward. "Dingle is quite taken." *Dingle?* "And Crumm finds her an excellent companion." *Crumm?* "And—"

"Stop. Just stop. Fia is mine and you know it."

Grant's golden lashes batted. "Yours?"

"Aye. I love her and she loves me. We are meant to be together."

"But she and Dingle would make such lovely children together."

A snort at his side captured his attention and he turned his head to find Fia awake and staring at him with those lovely blue-green eyes.

"Fia, darling," he said leaning down to press his lips to her hands. "Are you all right?"

"Did you say you loved me?"

He froze. Hell. He had. The hairs on his neck prickled. "That wasna the way I wanted to tell you."

"But do you?"

"Yes. Hell yes."

Her face broke into a smile. It had a mischievous mien about it. "How were you going to tell me?"

What? "I...ah...something romantic."

"Such as?"

Hell. He hadn't thought that far ahead. "Fia— Can we talk about that later?"

She put out a lip. It made him want to suckle it. "I suppose."

"For now, I must say, that is, I need to say…"

"Well?"

He sucked in a deep breath and rallied his courage and did the most terrifying thing he'd ever done. "Darling, you were right and I was wrong."

Her eyes widened. "Oh. *Do go on.*"

"I was so wrapped in the past I didn't even realize it was holding me immobile. I didn't realize I was using my guilt as an excuse to stop living, to avoid more pain. But when you left, everything became clear. I want you. I need you. And I don't care if having you in my life, in my heart, causes me pain, because the pain without you is unbearable." She didn't respond, but she did stroke his cheek, which he found encouraging. "So what do you say? Can you forgive me for being an idiot? Would you consider spending your life with me in a drafty old house in Dunbeath?"

"Darling," she said, leaning up to kiss him. "I would live with you in a hovel in Dunbeath."

"Really?"

"Aye."

"I own one of those too."

They laughed and kissed again and kissed and kissed until Grant felt compelled to clear his throat and remind them he was there. Damn and blast.

Daniel eased away and then helped Fia sit on the divan, settling himself next to her.

"You do realize you must ask for my blessing, don't you?" his erstwhile friend asked.

It was all Daniel could do not to plant him a facer.

Dinner that night was magnificent, and not only because Daniel had Fia, his Fia, by his side.

Grant had had the right of it, bringing all his friends together for a memorial on the first anniversary of the battle of Waterloo. They sat at the table and ate and drank, and lifted their cups in honor of all their fallen comrades. Then they all told stories of the lost men, stories that had them wavering between tears and uncontrollable laughter.

It was almost as though they were in the room, each and every one.

Somehow, through the sharing of their grief and anguish, the holes in their souls became a little less ragged.

It was only natural that the conversation would turn to the battle itself, and while Daniel dreaded reliving those hours, he knew it was necessary if he was to fully heal, to put it behind him.

Fia held his hand as the other men told of their experiences, the things they'd seen. Though, with respect to the ladies, they glossed over much. Through it all, her touch warmed him, made the memories bearable.

Although, when Crumm began talking about the moment they realized they were surrounded by the French lancers, when their men began to fall, he might have squeezed a little too hard. Still, she did not withdraw.

"I will never forget what you did then," Crumm said, turning to Daniel.

He blinked, and a shard of that familiar guilt skewered him. Heat prickled his neck. What had he done? Abandoned his honor, that's what he'd done.

"Aye." Dingle lifted his glass. "Without you we'd all be dead."

"To Sinclair."

"To Sinclair."

Daniel stared at them, one after the other. What the hell were they talking about? He'd run. He'd turned tail and run.

"Aye." Grant said, his attention locked onto his glass. He lifted it slowly and met Daniel's eye. "You saved us all." He turned to Fia. "He cut a swath through the French lancers, cleared a path for us to retreat."

"I...did?" He had no memory of that. No recollection whatsoever. All he remembered was the howling grief at seeing Lennox fall and a screaming panic to escape.

Crumm laughed. "Like a fooking Hun." He glanced at the ladies and winced. "Beg pardon."

"Never seen a man fight so fiercely," Dingle said. "You saved the entire company."

"Hell, one of them damn frogs gored him in the thigh and he just kept going," Crumm said. "Angel of Fury, some said."

"It was quite a sight." Grant poured himself another drink.

"I have no recollection of it."

Grant nodded. "Aye. And that is a mercy, I suppose."

The conversation went on. Men chatted about this and that, but Daniel was oblivious to it all. How could it be that he had remembered things so differently? And then he realized, it didn't matter.

What mattered, all that mattered, was that he was not such a tarnished soul after all. Aye, he had killed men that day, but—apparently—he'd saved lives too. The realization swelled within him, filled him, healed him.

He glanced at Fia to find her watching him with shining eyes. Her lips kicked up as their gazes tangled.

Ah. And he had her.

He had her love.

Life was beautiful indeed.

She leaned closer and her scent coiled around him, reached down into his gut and yanked. "Come to my room tonight," she whispered. Her tongue dabbed his ear and his cock lurched.

"I...what?"

"I've missed you."

He nearly jumped from his chair as a hand, a small, delicate, fragile hand, cupped his length. And squeezed.

"Say you'll come to my room."

Holy hell. "Damned straight I will."

The ladies retired shortly after that, but the men were in no mood to end their ruminations. Or their tippling. It was quite late when Daniel was able to break away, pleading exhaustion.

When he entered Fia's room—one that was inexplicably far from his own—she was sitting at the table by the window where her chess set was arranged, studying the pieces. She glanced up, but she didn't smile, as he expected her to. Her lip came out. "It took you long enough," she said.

He chuckled and came to her, dropping a kiss on her forehead. She smelled wonderful, of apples and cinnamon. His ardor stirred. "Grant wouldna let me go. No doubt he could read my intentions."

She sighed. "He is terribly overbearing. Worse than a father, I think."

"He cares for you." Though he'd led Daniel on a merry dance, he had finally given his blessing. Although, it hardly mattered if he had or not. Fia was his.

His.

He set his hand on her shoulder, tangled his fingers in her hair. Stroked her neck.

She glanced up at him with a hungry gaze and placed the knight she held in its starting position.

"Your set is complete," he said softly.

"Indeed it is."

He waved at the board. "Shall we play a game?"

"Chess?"

"Naturally."

She stood then and smiled at him, a smile that made heat whip through him. She wrapped her arms around him and pressed herself against him. "We can play chess any time. I have another game in mind."

She gave a little wiggle, one that made clear her intentions.

Another game?

Another game, indeed.

Also by Sabrina York

CONTEMPORARY

Stand Alone
Heartbreak on a Stick (Contemporary Romance)
Pool Man (Sexy Vacation Debacle)
Whipped (Contemporary Romance)
Fierce (One Night Stand, Decadent Publishing)
Snow Angels (Calendar Men Series from Decadent Publishing)

Stone Hard SEALs — Action Adventure Romance
Stone Hard SEALs (Action-Packed Military Romance Duet)
Guard Dog (Stone Hard SEALs/Hot SEALs Crossover)
Herding Cat (Stone Hard SEALs/Hot SEALs Crossover)
Hot Rod (Omega Team)

Stripped Down Cowboys (And Prequel Novellas)
Stud For Hire, Book 1
Cowboy to Command, Book 2
Spurred On, Book 3

Prequel Novellas
The Real McCoy Prequel Book 1
Come Hell or High Water Prequel Book 2
Protect and Serve — Cowboy Justice 12 Pack Prequel Book 3

Tryst Island Series — Steamy Contemporary Romance
Rebound Book 1
Dragonfly Kisses Book 2
Smoking Holt Book 3
Heart of Ash Book 4
Devlin's Dare Book 5
Parker's Passion Book 6

REGENCY

Stand Alone
Tarnished Honor

Untamed Highlanders!
Hannah and the Highlander Book 1
Susana and the Scot Book 2
Lana and the Laird Book 3

The Dundragon Time Travel Trilogy
Laird of her Heart Book 1
Her Hot Highlander Book 2 (Coming Soon)
His Highland Lass Book 3 (Coming Soon)

COLLECTIONS

Historical
Luscious — Seven Nights of Sin (Regency)

Cowboys
Protect and Serve — Cowboy Justice 12 Pack

Elite Metal/Action Adventure
Lithium's Rescue — Elite Metal Ghosts
Sterling's Seduction — Elite Metal Ghosts

About the Author

Her Royal Hotness, Sabrina York, is the New York Times and USA Today Bestselling author of hot, humorous stories for smart and sexy readers. Her titles range from sweet & sexy to scorching romance. Visit her webpage at www.sabrinayork.com to check out her books, excerpts and contests.

www.ingramcontent.com/pod-product-compliance
Lightning Source LLC
Chambersburg PA
CBHW071916220626
47052CB00002B/385